Where Texas society reigns supreme—
and appearances are everything.

CAST OF CHARACTERS

Cole Yardley was used to working alone. The last thing he needed or wanted to mess up his investigation was the interference of a *woman*, even if she just happened to be smart as a whip and sexier than sin.

Elise Campbell had sworn that she would never fall for a colleague. But "Caveman Cole Yardley" was bulldozing his way into her heart the same way he was trying to take over her investigation!

Ricky Mercado was sick of insinuations that he was involved with the cache of guns recently found at the Lone Star Country Club. Now he had federal agents breathing down his neck. If only he could wipe the slate clean and make a fresh start....

Dear Reader,

Experience passion and power in six brand-new, provocative titles from Silhouette Desire this July!

Begin with *Scenes of Passion* (#1519) by *New York Times* bestselling author Suzanne Brockmann. In this scintillating love story, a pretend marriage turned all too real reveals the torrid emotions and secrets of a former bad-boy millionaire and his prim heiress.

DYNASTIES: THE BARONES continues in July with *Cinderella's Millionaire* (#1520) by Katherine Garbera, in which a pretty pastry cook's red-hot passion melts the defenses of a brooding Barone hero. *In Bed with the Enemy*, (#1521) by rising star Kathie DeNosky, is the second LONE STAR COUNTRY CLUB title in Desire. In this installment, a lady agent and her lone-wolf counterpart bump more than heads during an investigation into a gun-smuggling ring.

What would you do if you were *Expecting the Cowboy's Baby* (#1522)? Discover how a plain-Jane bookkeeper deals with this dilemma in this steamy love story, the second Silhouette Desire title by popular Harlequin Historicals author Charlene Sands. Then see how a brokenhearted rancher struggles to forgive the woman who betrayed him, in *Cherokee Dad* (#1523) by Sheri WhiteFeather. And in *The Gentrys: Cal* (#1524) by Linda Conrad, a wounded stock-car driver finds healing love in the arms of a sexy, mysterious nurse, and the Gentry siblings at last learn the truth about their parents' disappearance.

Beat the summer heat with these six new love stories from Silhouette Desire.

Enjoy!

Melissa Jeglinski
Senior Editor, Silhouette Desire

Please address questions and book requests to:
Silhouette Reader Service
U.S.: 3010 Walden Ave., P.O. Box 1325, Buffalo, NY 14269
Canadian: P.O. Box 609, Fort Erie, Ont. L2A 5X3

In Bed with
the Enemy

KATHIE DeNOSKY

Silhouette
Desire

Published by Silhouette Books

America's Publisher of Contemporary Romance

Special thanks and acknowledgment are given to Kathie DeNosky for her contribution to the LONE STAR COUNTRY CLUB series.

 SILHOUETTE BOOKS

ISBN 0-373-76521-5

IN BED WITH THE ENEMY

Books by Kathie DeNosky

Silhouette Desire

Did You Say Married?! #1296
The Rough and Ready Rancher #1355
His Baby Surprise #1374
Maternally Yours #1418
Cassie's Cowboy Daddy #1439
Cowboy Boss #1457
A Lawman in Her Stocking #1475
In Bed with the Enemy #1521

KATHIE DeNOSKY

lives in her native southern Illinois with her husband, three children and two very spoiled dogs. Kathie's books have appeared on the Waldenbooks bestseller list. She enjoys going to rodeos, traveling to research settings for her books and listening to country music. You may write to Kathie at P.O. Box 2064, Herrin, IL 62948-5264 or e-mail her at kathie@kathiedenosky.com.

Dedication

I was thrilled when Silhouette invited me to be part of this series. Knowing very little about the duties of a FBI or an ATF agent, I embraced the challenge and learned all that I could about these two federal agencies. This story blends fact, fiction and a few creative liberties. By no means am I an expert on the FBI or the ATF.

Special thanks to Joan Marlow Golan and Mavis Allen for offering me the opportunity to write this book.
To Ann Major for being such a dear and allowing me to learn from one of the best. You're a true inspiration.
And last—but certainly not least—to Sheri WhiteFeather, a wonderfully talented author and deeply cherished friend, for being such a doll to work with. Thank you for the long talks and the shared laughter. Creating characters with you and brainstorming plots was sheer heaven.
I can't wait to do it again.

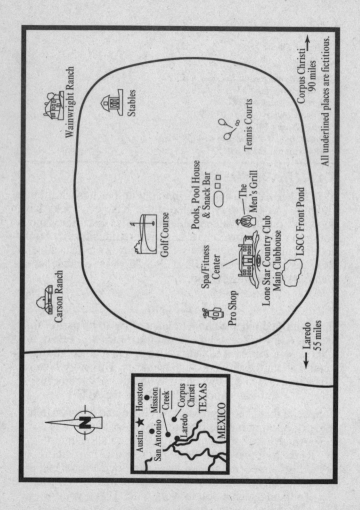

Wainwright Ranch

Stables

Tennis Courts

Pools, Pool House
& Snack Bar

The
Men's Grill

Golf Course

Carson Ranch

Spa/Fitness
Center

Lone Star Country Club
Main Clubhouse

LSCC Front Pond

Pro Shop

Corpus Christi
90 miles

All underlined places are fictitious.

Laredo
55 miles

N

Austin ★ Houston

San Antonio

Mission
Creek

Corpus
Christi

Laredo

TEXAS

MEXICO

One

"Haven't I had enough to deal with for one day?" Elise Campbell muttered when she missed the key-hole for the second time.

Waiting two hours for the judge to sign the court order had been a study in frustration. Then, having to listen to John Valente, the new head of the Mercado family, call her "doll" all afternoon made her feel as if she needed a shower. Now she couldn't see over the stack of files in her arms to fit the key into her door at the Mission Creek Inn. Thank goodness once she finally got inside, she could relax and be fairly certain that nothing more could go wrong.

Juggling her purse, the heavy stack of accounting records she'd just confiscated from Valente's office and a small pepperoni pizza, she made another stab at fitting the key into the lock. In hindsight, she wished she'd made two trips from the rental car to her room, instead of trying to carry it all at one time. But with the mid-August temperature well over a hundred degrees, all she'd been able to think about was getting back inside to collapse in the cool comfort of the air-conditioning.

When she finally heard the quiet click of the lock's release, she quickly turned the knob, stumbled into the room, kicked the door shut behind her and rushed over to dump everything on the desk. Shaking her arms to relieve the quivering in her strained muscles, she crossed the room to stand in front of the vent. The cool air blowing over her heated skin felt heavenly and she decided that after the day she'd had, she deserved a relaxing bath, then a glass of wine with her pizza before she started poring over the computer printouts.

Checking the connecting door between her room and the one next to it, she sighed heavily. The lock was broken. What else could go wrong?

When she checked in this morning, the innkeeper had given her the choice between the two rooms, so she knew the one next door was empty. But that didn't mean it would stay that way. Taking the chair from the desk, she jammed it under the doorknob. At least maybe it would slow someone down if they tried to enter her room without an invitation.

Twenty minutes later, she sat cross-legged in the middle of the queen-size bed, nibbling on a piece of pizza crust while she watched the six o'clock news. The weatherman promised that the rest of the month in south Texas was going to be a carbon copy of the past few days—hot. She glanced down at the shorts and tank top she'd pulled on after her bath. It was a shame she couldn't wear clothes like these to do her job, instead of tailored suits and panty hose.

Shrugging, Elise reached for the glass of wine she'd ordered from room service. She froze with the goblet halfway to her lips when she heard someone enter the room next to hers. Listening closely, she detected a single set of heavy footsteps crossing the room. Definitely a man. A dull thump followed by a succinct curse caused her eyes to widen. Either the man had dropped a large piece of luggage, or a body. By the phrases he was using, she wasn't sure which. But whoever the guy was on the other side of the wall, he definitely was *not* a happy camper.

Moving her 9 mm Glock within easy reach, she slid it out of the holster and released the safety. She wasn't thrilled that the lock on the door connecting their rooms was broken, but there wasn't anything she could do about that now. She glanced at the chair still propped under the knob. If the guy in the next room really wanted into her room, a lock wouldn't prevent him from gaining entry any more than the chair would. Locks only slowed criminals down, they didn't keep them out.

When she heard the door on his side of the wall open, she gripped the gun in her right hand, extended her arm, then cupped the butt end with her left hand. She wasn't the least bit surprised when the door on her side of the wall swung wide, shattering the chair as it crashed against the corner of the desk.

A very tall, extremely well-built man with short, dark-brown hair and piercing hazel eyes stood like a tree rooted to the spot. ''I want to know what the hell you think you're doing interfering in my case, Campbell,'' he demanded, paying absolutely no attention to the gun pointed at the middle of his black T-shirt.

''And I want to know what you think you're doing barging into my room without so much as knocking, Yardley,'' Elise asked calmly, lowering the gun. She engaged the safety, then holstered the firearm. ''Of course, that's the ATF's style, isn't it? Just storm in without the slightest thought about the consequences.''

''No more so than the FBI's style of sending a woman out in the field to do a man's job,'' he retorted.

Grinding her back teeth at the sexist barb, Elise refused to give him the satisfaction of knowing he'd touched a nerve. She smiled sweetly. ''I see you haven't changed since the last time I saw you. You're still Caveman Cole, the ATF's very own knuckle-dragging Neanderthal.''

He shrugged as he reached into the box on the desk to take a piece of pizza. ''Some things don't change. Your tongue's still as sharp as ever.'' His hazel eyes twinkling, he gave her an amused grin. ''But if you're wanting to know what my opinion is of female agents working in the field—''

''I already know all about them, Yardley,'' Elise interrupted as she unfolded her legs to sit on the side of the bed. ''And I could care less. The fact that my superiors have confidence in my abilities is all that matters.'' Laughing, she added, ''Your opinion certainly doesn't.''

She watched a muscle jerk along his lean jaw. Her

statement had irritated him. Good. She was pretty darned ticked off herself.

"When the spit hits the fan, the last thing a man needs is to be watching out for a woman," he said unapologetically. "Somebody could get hurt or killed."

"Oh, give me a break, Yardley. Female agents are just as competent as male agents."

Cole shook his head as he chewed the pizza. Women! Just because she'd gone through training, been issued a gun and awarded the same title as her male counterparts didn't mean she was capable of conducting high-priority investigations. And the Mercado crime family's connection to the smuggling ring funneling weapons into the tiny Central American country of Mezcaya was just such a case.

Distracted by thoughts of women holding jobs they weren't physically capable of doing, he was completely unprepared when she stood up and walked toward him. The sight of her long, slender legs made his mouth go as dry as a container of talcum powder. What in hell had her superiors been thinking when they assigned such a soft-looking, attractive female operative with the stakes this high?

What was her first name? Eloise? Eleanor? Eliza?

Whatever the hell it was, the FBI's Special Agent Campbell was not only the prickliest female he'd ever encountered, she had the best-looking legs he'd seen in ages. They were the kind of legs that a man dreamed of having wrapped around him when he sank himself—

Cole clenched his teeth and bit back a pithy curse. But when she walked past the air-conditioning vent on her way to the desk for another piece of pizza, he thought his eyes might just pop right out of his head. The cold air made her nipples peak and push against her hot-pink tank top.

Ah, hell. She wasn't wearing a bra. His lower body stirred as if to remind him that, although he didn't like noticing that little fact about her, it wasn't an unpleasant sight.

Shoving the last bite of the pizza slice into his mouth to keep from cussing a blue streak, he decided right then and there to take some vacation time after he wrapped up this case. What he needed was a few days with nothing more to concentrate on than a six-pack of ice-cold beer and a warm, willing woman. He knew for a fact that he'd been without female companionship too damn long if the sight of Campbell aroused him.

She wasn't just pretty, he thought grudgingly as he studied her flawless features. With her short auburn hair complementing her wide emerald eyes and peaches-and-cream complexion, she was actually a damn fine-looking woman. So why hadn't he noticed that when they worked parallel cases two years ago? She looked the same now as she had then. Of course, it had been winter and she'd been wearing pantsuits instead of shorts and a top that should be outlawed.

When his body tightened and his jeans suddenly felt a little too snug for comfort, Cole gritted his teeth and forced himself to remember who she was. This was the woman who not only started meddling in the case he was building against the Mercado family and their suspected gun-smuggling operation, she just plain rubbed him the wrong way every time he found himself in the same room with her.

"Well, do you?" she asked, giving him an expectant look.

Hell, he'd been so busy trying to figure out why he suddenly found her attractive, he had no idea what she was talking about. "What was the question again?"

She pointed to the splinters of wood at his feet. "Do you intend to see that the ATF reimburses the inn for that chair? Since you were the one who broke it, I don't think the FBI should be held responsible."

"Yeah, sure. Whatever." He bent down to pick up the pieces at the same time she did. When their heads collided, she went reeling backward and Cole had to act fast to keep her from falling on her sweet little rear. "Are you all right?"

"If I had any doubt before, I've got the proof now," she said, ruffling the soft-looking curls at her temple as she rubbed her head.

"What are you talking about?" How was a man supposed to know what a woman meant when she talked in circles?

"I've always suspected you were hardheaded." She quickly stepped away from him. "Now I know for sure. You are."

Cole might have laughed at her quick-witted response if he'd been able to draw a breath. The feel of her smooth, warm skin where he'd caught her arms had sent a jolt of electricity straight up his own arms to spread throughout his chest, and the peach scent of her newly washed hair had wrapped around him like a velvet cape.

He swallowed hard and rubbed his own head. They must have hit harder than he'd thought. Hell, he might even have a mild concussion. It was the only reason he could think of to explain *that* kind of reaction to her.

After he'd picked up what was left of the chair, he started for the door. "I'll be back as soon as I put this in the Dumpster. Then we'll talk about your investigation."

She cocked one perfectly arched eyebrow. "Oh, really?"

Grinning, Cole opened the door leading into the hall. "Yep. We're going to set some kind of boundary to keep you from blowing my case."

"*Me* blowing your case?" She propped her fists on her shapely hips and tapped her bare foot on the carpet. "What about *you* jeopardizing mine?"

He shrugged. "It won't matter. I'll have Ricky Mercado and the rest of his family in custody and indicted for gun smuggling before you even get started."

When he closed the door, he laughed out loud at the unladylike phrase he heard coming from the other side.

Elise sat with her back propped against the headboard of the bed, thinking about what had happened when Caveman Cole caught her to prevent her fall. His large hands on her bare arms had made every nerve in her body spark to life and sent a wave of goose bumps skipping over her skin. And that confused her.

She'd never had that kind of reaction to him before.

Far from it. Two years ago, when they'd conducted parallel investigations on a case similar to the Mercado family's, she'd ended each day so angry, so utterly and completely frustrated by his chauvinistic attitude, that each night she'd bought a quart of double-fudge, chocolate-chunk ice cream and eaten the whole carton. But who wouldn't be upset by his antiquated views of what careers women should and shouldn't have?

Caveman Cole had made it perfectly clear that he thought women had absolutely no business doing anything but staying home to cook, clean and bear children. Period.

Elise had no problem with staying home, if that was what a woman wanted. She did, however, have a *big* problem with a man telling her what her choices should be. She had a mind of her own, thank you very much, and she was perfectly capable of deciding for herself what she wanted to do with her life.

She sighed. But as irritating as it had been to be around Caveman Cole, that case had garnered her a commendation and gained her the reputation of being one of the best in the Bureau for finding a paper trail where none seemingly existed. Unfortunately, it had also caused her to put on an extra ten pounds.

When the Caveman strolled back through the door connecting his room to hers, she frowned. The man was insufferable and the most arrogant soul she'd ever met.

"Don't you ever knock?" She shook her head. "No need to answer that. You being an ATF agent, I don't suppose you do."

"Like the FBI is any better about knocking when

they make a raid,'' he said, plopping down in the armchair across the room.

She sighed. "This isn't getting us anywhere."

"At least we agree on that," he said, nodding. He leaned forward, propped his forearms on his knees and loosely clasped his hands between his knees. "The way I see it, we can play this one of two ways."

"And what would they be?" If he thought he was going to take over her investigation, he'd better think again.

"You can tell me what you're investigating and I'll let you know if that will hurt my case." When she started to tell him she'd do no such thing, he held up a hand. "Or, I can tell you what to leave alone."

Elise shook her head. "Fat chance, Yardley. You're not telling me what to do. But you'll find out anyway, so I might as well tell you. I seized the accounting records of the Mercados' trucking and produce companies this afternoon."

"Going after the money angle, huh?"

"It's a place to start."

"You do know you've got the doctored version of their books?" he asked. "The real records are tucked away in some vault somewhere."

"Of course. I wasn't born yesterday, Yardley." She studied his handsome face. The fact that she found him even remotely attractive was as irritating as it was disconcerting. "Tomorrow I'll get court orders to seize the accounts of Ricky Mercado, his late uncle, Carmine Mercado, and the late Frank Del Brio. If there are any discrepancies, I'll find them."

"Then what are you going to do?" he asked, looking deceptively relaxed. He was good at fishing for information. She'd give him that much.

But she knew better than to trust him. "Why don't you come right out and ask how I'm going to conduct my investigation, Yardley?"

He grinned. "Fair enough. How are you going to bring the Mercados down?"

"So far, neither the Bureau nor the ATF have been able to prove the connection between the guns leaving Texas and the ones being smuggled into Mezcaya," she said, shrugging. "I intend to find the paper trail proving that the Mercados are the ones selling the guns, and if my instincts are right, they're using their trucking company to transport them into Mezcaya."

"Good luck," he said, leaning back in the chair.

She smiled. "Now it's your turn."

"My turn?"

"Yes, your turn." She narrowed her eyes. "You're going to tell me how you intend to prove the Mercados are behind this."

"Sorry, Campbell," he said, rising to his feet. "I don't reveal my moves before I make them. And I for damn sure don't work with women."

"Oh, so that's the way it's going to be, huh?" Elise rose from the bed to stand toe-to-toe with him. Unfortunately, she was a good six inches shorter than he was and had to tilt her head back to look him squarely in the eye. "We're going to keep our discoveries about the investigation separate?"

"That's right, sweetheart." His cocky grin made her want to punch him. "I work alone during this phase of a case."

"Fair enough, Caveman," she said, smiling.

"You've heard the last of the way I plan to conduct my investigation." She walked over to the door connecting their two rooms. "And just so you're warned. My name is Elise or Campbell, not 'sweetheart.' If you ever call me that again, I might not be so cautious about firing my gun the next time you come barging into my room."

Shrugging, he started through the door, but turned back to cup her cheek with his palm. "I'll stop calling you sweetheart when you stop calling me Caveman."

The heat from his hand spread down her neck to her torso and beyond. She took a deep breath. It wasn't a good feeling. It wasn't. Maybe if she keep repeating it, she'd start to believe that it was true.

"I want to thank you, *Caveman.*"

"For what, *sweetheart?*"

"I thought my day couldn't possibly get any worse than it was this afternoon." She gave him a smile that she hoped set his teeth on edge. "But in the past hour and a half, you've proven how wrong I was, and just how *bad* it could get."

Laughing, he had the audacity to wink at her before he dropped his hand and walked into his room.

Her anger close to the boiling point, Elise slammed the door on her side and barely resisted the urge to stomp her foot.

Cole walked over to turn on the television in the corner. Campbell's name was Elise. Surely he'd heard it when they worked the El Paso case two years ago. Why hadn't he remembered it?

Sitting on the end of the bed, he pulled off his boots, then stared off into space.

Elise. It was a soft, sweet-sounding name, and suited her perfectly. Her smooth skin beneath his palms had felt like fine satin when he'd caught her to keep her from falling, and when he'd cupped her cheek he'd been tempted to press his lips to hers to see if they tasted as sweet as they looked.

He cursed and shook his head. He must be losing it. This was Campbell, the FBI's "go-to" girl. The woman with a pain-in-the-ass attitude and a razor-sharp tongue.

But that was no excuse for the way he'd reacted to her. The way he'd always reacted to her.

He'd never been in the habit of baiting a woman the way he did whenever he was around her. On the contrary. He had the utmost respect for women. They were soft, gentle and deserved a man's consideration, as well as his protection. And it was a damn good thing his old man wasn't alive to hear about the exchange. Gunnery Sergeant Albert Yardley would kick Cole's butt from here to yonder for talking to a woman the way he had spoken to Campbell.

Thinking about his father, Cole smiled. Gunny had been a walking contradiction when it came to his views on the fairer sex.

From the time Cole had been old enough to listen, the man had lectured him about where a woman's place should be in the world. "Keep 'em barefoot and pregnant, boy, and you'll never have to worry about 'em bein' in the way when the spit hits the fan." But at the same time, his father thought a man should place a woman on a pedestal and give her his undivided attention and complete respect. And Cole suspected if his mother hadn't died when he was four, he'd have had a whole houseful of brothers and sisters.

But he hadn't had that. He'd been raised by a crusty, career marine gunnery sergeant, and learned early on not to get too attached to people or places. An unusual sense of loneliness filled his chest.

Cole shook off the feeling as he rose to pull off his T-shirt and jeans. "It's no wonder you're screwed up, Yardley."

But long after he'd taken his shower and climbed into bed, Cole stared at the ceiling, thinking about his exchange with his auburn-haired rival. He'd never met a woman he enjoyed verbally sparring with as much as he did with Campbell. She was one of the most intelligent, quick-witted women he'd ever met, and the sparkle of anger in her emerald eyes when she was reading him the riot act had been too tempting to resist.

Her spirit, and drive to be the best, were admirable traits in a male agent. But not in a female operative. Those were the very qualities about her that made her volatile.

Cole punched his pillow and rolled over to his side. Campbell wasn't the type to run from trouble. If anything, she would be the first to sink her teeth into a dangerous investigation and exhaust all possibilities before she let go.

He knew because he recognized it all too well. It was the same way he carried out his own job.

Two

The next afternoon, as Cole got out of his rented SUV, Ricky Mercado walked out onto his front porch, leaned his shoulder against one of the support posts and crossed his booted feet at the ankles. His relaxed stance didn't fool Cole one damn bit. He was the last person Mercado wanted to see.

"Back again, Yardley?"

"Yep." Cole grinned. He had a feeling that under different circumstances, he and Mercado could have been friends. But given the nature of his job and Ricky's background, it was unlikely now. "Just thought I'd let you know I'm still around."

Mercado laughed, but the spark of irritation in his dark brown eyes hinted at his true feelings about seeing Cole again. "Like you'll let me forget."

"How do you like your new place?"

"It'll do. I've got an old raccoon living under the back porch that doesn't care much for my moving here, but he can hiss and spit all he wants. I'm here to stay." Mercado uncrossed his feet and straightened to his full six foot three inch height. "Why don't you cut to the chase, Yardley."

Cole nodded. That was one thing he and Mercado had in common. Neither one of them minced words. "Fair enough. You've been going to the country club a lot lately."

"I paid a chunk of money for that membership. I figure on getting my money's worth."

"You know about the guns being found in one of the maintenance sheds?" Cole asked, watching for any sign that Mercado might be hiding something.

Mercado gave nothing away. "I'd have to be blind, deaf and dumb as hell not to have heard the news. You can't swing a dead armadillo in Mission Creek without hitting somebody who isn't talking about it."

"Do you have any idea who might have stashed them there?"

"Nope."

"Would you tell me if you did?"

"Sure."

Cole didn't believe him for a minute. "Do you think Valente is involved?"

A muscle jerked along Mercado's jaw and Cole could tell he'd touched a nerve. "You'll have to ask the SOB yourself. I have no idea what's going on inside. And I don't care." His expression hard, Mercado added, "I've told you before. I quit. I'm not associated with the family anymore, and I don't know what they're up to."

"That's what you keep telling me."

"If you're smart, you'll start to believe me and turn your investigation where it will do some good."

Cole wasn't surprised when Mercado became defensive about his involvement with his infamous family. They'd played out this scenario before.

"If you hear anything—"

"Yeah. I know. You'd appreciate me letting you know." With that, Mercado turned, walked back into the old house he was renovating, and slammed the door.

Cole checked his watch, got back into the SUV and headed into Mission Creek. He had roughly thirty minutes to get across town to the Lone Star Country Club for his meeting with Phillip Westin.

Westin had been Ricky Mercado's commanding officer and knew as much about him as the other marines who'd served with Mercado in the 14th Unit. Several of them lived in and around Mission Creek, and some of them even grew up with him. Yet, most of them had their doubts that Mercado had severed all ties with his family. Some had even gone so far as to say they believed Mercado's insistence that he'd gone legit was a cover-up for some kind of illegal activity. Only his brother-in-law, Luke Callaghan, and Phillip Westin had professed to believe that Mercado was on the up-and-up—that he was trying to get his life together and go straight.

But there were several things about Ricky Mercado and his story that bothered Cole. A lot.

Mercado had been on the rescue team sent to get Westin out of the tiny Central American country of Mezcaya. A hotbed of corruption, and in serious danger of being taken over by the terrorist group El Jefé, Mezcaya had suffered years of fighting and unrest. But after Mercado's mission to help save Westin, there had been a dramatic increase in the amount of automatic weapons and high-tech ordnance used by El Jefé. That alone was enough to raise a red flag the size of Rhode Island with the ATF's intelligence source.

But when a stash of M16s, along with grenades and handheld rocket launchers were discovered in one of the maintenance sheds on the grounds of the Lone Star Country Club, it had become a foregone conclusion that the Mercados were somehow involved. Several higher-ups in the family, including Ricky, had bought memberships in the exclusive club, giving them unlimited access to the grounds.

Coincidence? Not likely.

Cole turned the SUV onto the blacktop driveway leading up to the clubhouse, bypassed the valet parking at the entrance and pulled into the self-parking area at the side of the main building. With the stifling heat bouncing off the asphalt, he would have just as soon paid one of the valets to park the damn thing, but he could just imagine the shade of red his boss's face would turn if he handed the man a receipt for the ATF to pay for it.

Chuckling at the mental image, he steered the Explorer between a black Mercedes and a red Porsche, killed the engine, then opened the driver's-side door and came damn close to smacking Campbell right square in the face with it. Where the hell had she come from? She hadn't been standing there when he pulled into the parking space only moments ago.

When he slammed the door and locked it with the keyless remote, he turned to face her. Her trim black skirt, matching jacket and white blouse made her look ultraconservative, extremely professional and thoroughly unapproachable. Whether he was happy about it or not, he had to admit he liked the way she looked in shorts and a tank top a whole lot better.

She frowned. "I should have known it was you."

"Good afternoon to you too, Campbell," he said cheerfully.

She started to step around him, but with the cars parked so closely together, there wasn't enough room. "Will you please stand aside so I can get by, Yardley?"

"Sure," he said, grinning as he flattened himself against the SUV's door.

In order for her to get past him, she had to turn sideways. "Why couldn't you have just walked out ahead of me?"

"That wouldn't have been the gentlemanly thing to do," he answered as she squeezed by. The front of her body brushed against the front of his and a jolt of electricity as powerful as if he'd grabbed hold of a 220-volt wire coursed through him. He heard her sharp intake of breath, felt her go very still, indicating she'd felt it, too.

"Since when have you been worried about being a gentleman?" she asked, preceding him from between the vehicles. To his satisfaction, she sounded a little short of air.

"I'm always a gentleman."

She started walking toward the clubhouse. "Yeah. Right."

"Hey, where's the fire?" he asked when he had to hurry to catch up to her. "You have a hot lead you're following up on?"

"Like I'd tell you if I did." She laughed as she walked swiftly across the parking lot toward the sidewalk leading up to the clubhouse. "You were the one who made it clear our investigations were going to be kept separate."

"Yes, but—"

She stopped to look up at him. "But nothing, Yardley. You said, and I quote, 'I work alone during this phase of a case.' Did you not?"

"That's true, but I'm not above listening if you've got something to share."

The sparkle of anger in her pretty green eyes was back, along with a good amount of righteous indignation, and Cole found himself as fascinated by her today as he'd been last night. With her soft auburn curls stirring in the light breeze, he didn't think he'd seen her look more attractive either.

"You are without a doubt the most arrogant, infuriating man I've ever met," she said, shaking her head.

"Yeah, I probably am." Grinning, he shrugged. "But I look real good in a black ATF T-shirt and ball cap."

"What does that have to do with—" She shook her head. "Never mind. It doesn't matter. I really don't care to hear your caveman reasoning."

"There you go calling me a caveman again, *sweetheart*."

"Don't call me that."

"Don't call me Caveman."

"I didn't. I referred to your reasoning as that of a caveman. There's a difference." She grinned suddenly. "But I suppose in your case, it is only a matter of semantics."

He felt as if he'd been punched in the gut at the sweet smile curving her lips. "You know, Campbell. With all your references to cavemen, if I didn't know better, I'd think you're trying to get me to throw you over my shoulder and haul you off to my den."

Cole laughed out loud when she made a growling sound in the back of her throat, turned and marched into the building.

Elise plopped down in a plushly padded, wrought-iron chair at a table with a bright-yellow and white umbrella. Looking out over the rolling lawns of the golf course, she took several deep breaths in an effort to get herself under control before meeting with the head groundskeeper. She was so angry with herself for engaging in another battle of wits with Caveman Cole that she felt ready to scream. Why did she let him get to her? Why didn't she just ignore him?

Sighing, she leaned back in the chair and watched a group of golfers in the distance take their tee shots. If she was completely honest with herself, she'd have to admit that their verbal sparring wasn't what had her so upset. It was the sizzling awareness she'd felt for Cole Yardley as a man that frustrated her more than anything else. How could she possibly find anything about the man attractive? And why?

She didn't even like him. He was too arrogant, too sure of himself. And his attitude concerning female agents was not only antiquated, it was inexcusable. If he had his way, the women's movement would be set back by a good fifty years. Maybe even a hundred.

But when she'd brushed past him in the parking lot, the feel of his strong, hard body against hers had made her knees go weak. Then, when he'd stopped her to inquire about her lead in the investigation, she'd noticed how handsome he was, how his engaging smile caused her stomach to flutter.

He'd looked good wearing the tan sports jacket, black T-shirt and jeans. In fact, that was part of the problem. He'd looked too good to her.

For some men, a sports jacket and jeans were casual, but she suspected it was about as formal as Yardley dressed. In fact, today was the first time she'd seen him wearing something other than a black ATF T-shirt, jeans and boots. She compared both images in her mind and decided he looked good in both, but in a different way.

The tan sports jacket had emphasized his wide shoulders and brought out the highlights in his dark-brown hair and hazel eyes. But it also hid a lot that his ATF shirt showed off. Last night when he'd caught her after they'd bumped heads, she'd noticed how his T-shirt fit him like a second skin, how the knit stretched over well-defined pectoral muscles and strong, well-developed biceps.

A shiver snaked up her spine. What was wrong with her? She wasn't in the least bit interested in ATF Agent Yardley. Aside from the fact that she had little tolerance for overly confident hotshots, she had a golden rule to never mix business with pleasure. She never dated anyone she worked with. Ever.

"I'm sorry to have kept you waiting, Ms. Campbell," a man of about fifty said as he walked up to the table. Dressed in a khaki work shirt and pants with grass stains on the knees, this had to be her two o'clock appointment. "I was called away to check a water hazard over by the thirteenth hole." Offering his hand, he smiled. "I'm Carl Estrada, the head groundskeeper here at the Lone Star."

Grateful the man had interrupted her disturbing thoughts about Caveman Cole, she shook his hand. "Thank you for taking the time to speak with me, Mr. Estrada." She motioned to the chair across from her. "Please have a seat. I promise not to keep you too long."

When he'd seated himself, he shook his head. "I'll be more than happy to answer any questions you have. But I'm not sure that I'll be able to tell you anything that I haven't already told Agent Yardley."

Taking a pad of paper and pen from her shoulder bag, Elise nodded tersely. So, Caveman Cole had beat her to an interview with a witness. This would be the last time that happened.

"I understand, Mr. Estrada. But there might be something I ask that Agent Yardley didn't mention." Reviewing her questions, she smiled in an effort to put the man at ease. "I've been told you were the one who found the weapons in one of the equipment sheds."

"That's right." He pointed across the lawn to a group of buildings several hundred yards away. "It had been empty for some time and I was checking to see if there would be room to store all the new gardening equipment I'd ordered." He paused a moment, then continued. "What I found was the entire building packed full of wooden gun crates."

"Is there an access road leading to the sheds, Mr. Estrada?" Elise asked, praying she'd come up with something that Yardley hadn't.

"Yes, ma'am. But it's only used by employees and delivery trucks."

"What kinds of deliveries?" Elise asked curiously, wondering if Caveman Cole had pursued this angle.

Carl Estrada shrugged. "Mainly items for the Pro Shop, gardening and lawn equipment, and occasionally, when something big is coming up like the summer festival in just a few days, we store the extra nonperishable supplies needed for the restaurants and bars."

Elise perked up immediately. This just might be the lead she was looking for. "How are these deliveries made for the extra restaurant stock?"

"Usually they're trucked in by 18-wheelers," he said, nodding toward the access road. "In fact, here comes another delivery now. Would you like to walk over there and check things out?"

"I'd like that very much," she said, smiling. "Do you keep a log of incoming deliveries, Mr. Estrada?"

"Sure do." He nodded as they walked across the lawn. "I have it in my office down at the maintenance barn."

Knowing she could get a court order for the information, but hoping that route wouldn't be necessary, she asked, "Would you mind if I made copies of the last few months' entries?"

"Not at all," Carl said. "In fact, I have a copy machine in my office, if you'd like to use it."

Elise smiled again. "Thank you, Mr. Estrada. I think I'll do just that."

Through the window beside the table where he sat with Phillip Westin in the Men's Grill, Cole caught sight of Campbell walking across the lawn with Carl Estrada. What was she up to this time? Didn't she realize he'd already gone through those sheds with a fine-tooth comb, looking for any evidence left behind by whoever put the weapons there?

Cole grinned. She was a couple of days late on looking into that end of the investigation. He'd talked with Carl and inspected the sheds yesterday.

But as he watched her walk beside the grounds-keeper, Cole enjoyed the slight sway of her shapely hips, the elegance of her long, slender legs. Damn, the woman had legs that could easily cause a traffic jam.

"Like what you see, Yardley?" Phillip Westin asked, his silver-gray eyes twinkling as he grinned.

Cole shook his head. "Uh...not really," he lied. "I'm just wondering what she thinks she'll find out there. I combed those sheds for evidence the other day."

"Ah, a little friendly rivalry between the ATF and the FBI." Westin's grin widened, indicating that he didn't believe a word of Cole's excuse.

"Something like that," Cole muttered. He cleared his throat and reached for his beer. "Now, what were you saying about Mercado?"

Westin's expression suddenly turned serious. "I said I believe Ricky. He says he's backed out of the family business. That's good enough for me."

"What makes you think he's telling the truth?" Cole asked carefully. It was clear the man was convinced of Mercado's innocence. Cole wanted to know why.

"Any commanding officer in the Marine Corps worth a damn knows his men. Nine times out of ten, he knows when they're lying." Westin took a long draw from the beer in his hand. Placing the empty long-neck bottle on the table with a thump, he looked Cole square in the eye. "Mercado says he's gone straight, and from everything I've seen, he has."

Cole nodded. "He's been investing in real estate. From all indications, at least that part of the story is on the up-and-up."

"Like I said, I believe Mercado."

Deciding it was time to stop beating around the bush, Cole stated what bothered him the most about Mercado. "He was being groomed by his late uncle to assume control of the family, but Frank Del Brio was the one to take over when Carmine died."

Westin nodded. "But Ricky felt differently about the mob after Carmine died. Hell, I'm not real sure he was ever for it, but it damn sure wasn't long after that before he decided he had to get out." Westin leaned forward. "Then when Del Brio got killed, John Valente took the reins of the organization."

"Did Ricky turn it down, or was there a power struggle?" Cole asked, feeling as if he might be on to something. "I know there was bad blood between Del Brio and Mercado."

"Ricky never talked about it. I didn't ask." Westin shook his head. "We've always had an unspoken understanding about his family's activities. The less I know about what's going on with them, the better."

"That's probably the safest way to handle your friendship with Mercado," Cole agreed. He swallowed the last of his beer. "Speaking of safe, Wainwright said that you haven't had any more notes on slaughtered cattle for a while."

Westin's expression turned grim at the mention of the trouble he'd had lately. "No, that stopped about three weeks ago."

"If it will make you and your wife feel any better, I'm pretty sure the heat got to be too much for Gonzalez and he hightailed it back to Mezcaya."

Westin ran a frustrated hand through his dark hair, his eyes burning with pure fury at the mention of Xavier Gonzalez, the young El Jefé terrorist who held Westin responsible for his father's death. "If the bastard's smart, he'll stay there."

Cole didn't blame Westin in the least for the way he felt about the little jungle rat. Gonzalez had cost him several head of prime breeding stock, as well as running Westin's wife, Celeste, off the road and almost killing her before they were married.

The whole time he'd been sitting at the table with Phillip Westin, Cole had been surreptitiously glancing out the window to see when Campbell started back toward the clubhouse. Westin wasn't telling him anything that he hadn't told him before, and Cole knew the man had said all he intended to say on the subject of Ricky Mercado.

The moment he spotted her coming toward the clubhouse, Cole rose to his feet and extended his hand. "Thanks for meeting with me, Westin. I appreciate your time."

"Sorry that I couldn't be more help, Yardley." Westin shook Cole's hand and grinned. "But I'll tell you the same thing the next time you ask. Ricky isn't involved in any of the Mercados' dealings. I'd stake my life on it."

Cole nodded. "Time will tell."

When he reached for the check, Westin was faster. Grabbing the slip of paper, he shook his head and reached for his wallet. "If you stop to pay the tab, you'll miss her." He looked out the window at Campbell walking across the lawn toward the patio. "And that's one lady I don't think any man would want to miss."

"You're married. Remember?" Cole reminded tersely. Now where the hell had that come from?

Westin laughed. "Happily married! But I'm not blind."

The grin on Westin's face caused anger to burn in Cole's gut. And he couldn't for the life of him figure out why. He had absolutely no interest in Campbell. Zip. Zero. Nada.

"You'd better hurry, or she'll be long gone, Yardley."

Without another word, Cole turned and hurried to the exit of the Men's Grill with the sound of Phillip Westin's hearty laughter ringing in his ears.

Three

Elise stood on the enormous veranda of the Lone Star's clubhouse, digging through her shoulder bag for the key to her rental car. Why did the dumb thing always sink to the bottom of her purse? Just as her fingers closed around the key ring wedged beneath her checkbook and the leather case containing her FBI shield, she sensed that someone had come to stand beside her.

"Good afternoon, doll."

The skin along the back of her neck immediately felt as if it crawled at the sound of John Valente's voice. "Good afternoon, Mr. Valente," she said without looking at him.

She'd decided the first time she met John Valente, the new head of the Mercado crime family, that he probably gave his own mother the creeps. He was just that loathsome.

Tall and muscular, with short black hair and an olive complexion, John Valente was a dark, imposing figure, with rough features and a sneering smile. He had a crooked nose, indicating that it had been broken several times, a three-inch white scar running from his temple to his right cheekbone and several deep lines creasing his forehead. But those weren't the traits that bothered her the most about him.

Glancing up, she met his hooded gaze and a shudder of apprehension slithered up her spine. Each time she'd looked into his fathomless, dark-brown eyes, she'd been left with the feeling that the man had no integrity, no conscience, no soul.

"You aren't leaving are you, Ms. Campbell?" Valente asked, his gravelly voice sending a chill shimmering over her skin.

"That's Agent Campbell. And, yes, I am."

She started to walk away, but his hand at her elbow stopped her. "Please, won't you stay and join me for a drink?"

Even though she had gone through extensive training in self-defense, she had to fight the urge to keep from drawing away from him. "I can't. I'm on duty, Mr. Valente. Now, if you'll excuse me."

"There you are." At the sound of Cole Yardley's familiar voice, she and Valente both turned to watch him walking through the front doors of the clubhouse. "I've been looking for you, sweetheart."

Great. Now she had Caveman Cole to spar with as well as fending off this snake. What could she have possibly done to deserve having to deal with these two?

"Yardley." Valente's voice suddenly held a hard edge.

"Hello, Valente." Yardley walked up to put his arm around her waist, then drew her to his side.

She sucked in a sharp breath. "What do you think—"

"I see you've met Agent Campbell," he said, cutting her off.

Valente dropped his hand from her elbow, but she noticed he balled it into a tight fist at his side. "Yes, we had the pleasure of meeting yesterday afternoon. I only wish it had been under different, more pleasant, circumstances."

"I'm sure you do," Yardley said, his voice just as terse. His arm tightened around her when Valente sent a leering smile her way. If she didn't know better, she'd think Yardley was sending some kind of proprietary signal to Valente. Turning to her, he asked, "Are you ready to leave, sweetheart?"

"I can't believe—"

"I've got the keys to the car right here," Yardley interrupted, holding up a keyless remote. Before she could take him to task over using the familiarity, he steered her down the sidewalk, at the same time calling over his shoulder, "See you around, Valente."

"What was that all about?" she demanded, starting to pull away from him.

"Just play along, Campbell," he said, holding her firmly against him as he guided her toward the SUV. "Valente's still standing on the porch watching us."

"And that's supposed to mean something?"

"He's watching to see if we leave together." Yardley pushed a button on the remote to unlock the doors.

"At some point, he's going to discover we aren't."

"Wrong. He's going to see us get in my car and leave."

"No, he isn't."

In definite caveman mode, Yardley had the audacity to take her into his arms. "Yes, he is."

"What do you think you're—"

"I'm making sure Valente knows to leave you alone," he said, lowering his head.

She started to tell him that she could take care of herself, but the moment his mouth covered hers, Elise forgot whatever she'd been about to say. Cole's kiss was slow and thoughtful, as if he was acquainting himself with her.

But when he traced her lips with his tongue, then slipped inside to caress the sensitive inner recesses of her mouth, Elise stopped wondering why he wanted Valente to think they were together, and concentrated on the way Cole's kiss made her feel.

A warmth like nothing she'd ever felt began to course through her veins, heating her in a way that made her knees wobble. He lifted the tail of her suit jacket to splay his hands across her back and pull her more fully to him. A fluttering swirl deep in her lower stomach began to form. But when he reached down to cup her bottom and drew her to him the feel of his hard arousal tightened the sensation and caused the most interesting tingling to pull at her lower body.

Her pulse took off at breakneck speed and alarm bells began to clang inside her head as panic began to build. This was Caveman Cole. A man who was working the same case she was on, and who she might have to work closely with again.

Pushing against him, she managed to put a bit of space between them, but he continued to hold her close as he broke the kiss. "That wasn't a good idea," she said, hating how breathless she sounded.

The grin he gave her caused her toes to curl in her black pumps. "Sure it was. Now, get in the truck. Valente is still watching."

"What does that matter?" How was she supposed to think with his arousal still pressed to her lower body? Her mind came to a screeching halt. His arousal?

"I want him to back off and leave you alone." Cole met Campbell's confused gaze. "Now, smile like you're having a good time and get in the truck."

The determined smile she gave him wasn't what he'd had in mind. "No."

"I said get in the truck, sweetheart," he repeated through clenched teeth.

"I said no, Caveman."

Her defiance irritated the hell out of him. He should have known she'd argue with him. The woman was as stubborn as he was. "I swear, if you don't get in this truck, I'll kiss you again."

Her pretty, green eyes narrowed. "You wouldn't dare."

Resting his forehead against hers, he kissed the tip of her nose and pressed his lower body more intimately to hers. "Try me."

She stared at him for several long seconds, then pulling from his arms, opened the passenger door of the SUV and climbed inside. The glare she sent his way could have wilted a cactus, and it was all he could do to keep from laughing out loud at the colorful phrase she muttered just before slamming the Explorer's door.

Taking a deep breath, he started around the back of the vehicle. He hadn't been prepared for the impact of that kiss. My God, the woman had the sweetest lips he'd ever tasted, and he was still fighting the urge to throw her over his shoulder, find a secluded place and love her senseless.

But when he glanced toward the porch, the last traces of his desire vanished. Valente was still standing there watching, taking in the scene Cole had just staged with Campbell, like some kind of voyeur. Even though Cole wanted the man to get the message to leave her alone, nothing would have pleased him more than the pleasure of burying his fist in Valente's leering face.

When Cole slid behind the steering wheel, Campbell looked as if she intended to take a strip or two off his hide. "Before you get started, hear me out, Campbell. Unless you want to be fending off Valente the whole time you're trying to conduct your investigation, you'll let him think that you and I are more than just co-workers."

She surprised him by laughing. "You are without a doubt a caveman in every sense of the word, Yardley. Do you honestly think I can't handle a creep like Valente?"

"I'm sure you think you can." Cole backed the SUV from the parking space, then steered the Explorer onto the country club's blacktop driveway.

"But Valente is a man without many, if any, redeeming qualities."

"And you think if he has the idea that you and I are—" she paused as if searching for the right word "—involved, it will stop him from interfering in my investigation?"

"Not exactly." Cole turned onto the main road leading back toward Mission Creek. "But I know his type. He doesn't see you as a federal agent. All he sees is an attractive woman he'll try to manipulate. Every time you turn around he'll be in your face, trying to find out what you've learned so he can try to divert your investigation."

"Give me more credit than to fall for something that obvious, Yardley."

Cole glanced over at her. "Do you honestly think that little scene on the porch back there at the Lone Star was a chance meeting? That Valente just happened to be dropping by the clubhouse as you walked out the front door?"

"I hadn't thought about it," she said, frowning.

"Let me assure you, it wasn't," he said flatly. "He's got his goons watching every move you make, reporting back to him where you are and who you're with." Cole pulled the SUV to a stop in the inn's parking lot. "Today was my way of letting Valente know that if he doesn't back off, he'll have me to contend with."

Elise stared at Cole, not quite sure what to say. If she didn't know better, she'd think he was trying to protect her from Valente as a man protects a woman he's interested in, as well as the integrity of her investigation. Ridiculous. Caveman Cole didn't even like her. Why would he be concerned about her?

"I think I'm capable of handling a snake like John Valente."

"I know you think you are," he said, killing the engine. "But what is your specialty with the Bureau?"

"You worked with me two years ago. You know that I have a master's degree in accounting."

He nodded. "My point exactly. The majority of your time is spent in an office with your nose stuck in computer printouts or some other kind of accounting records." Reaching out, he cupped her chin in his palm and the warmth from his hand sent a wave of heat straight to her toes. "You don't have the experience out in the field that I have, and you're not used to dealing with vermin like Valente. I am."

She pulled back from his touch to keep from leaning into it. "And how else am I supposed to gain this invaluable experience if I don't get out of the office and interact with Valente's kind?"

"Dammit, woman! You haven't been paying attention to a word I've said, have you?"

He got out of the Explorer, but before he could round the front of the vehicle, she breathed a sigh of relief and opened the passenger door herself. The caveman was back. Thank heavens. She was much more comfortable embroiled in a verbal battle with Caveman Cole than she was dealing with Cole Yardley, the man whose kiss made her insides feel like warm pudding.

"This is the very reason I won't work with a woman," he muttered as he walked up to put his hands on the fender of the SUV, trapping her between his arms. Leaning forward until their noses almost touched, he added, ''Female agents think they're just as capable as men in any field situation. They're not. But guess who'll end up getting shot while he's trying to save the woman's ass?''

''Oh, give me a break, Caveman. Do you honestly think that women agents are that incompetent?''

''I didn't say they're incompetent,'' he argued. ''What I'm saying is that men like Valente don't play by the rules, and women like you aren't prepared to deal with them.''

''I don't think Valente poses that big of a threat to me.''

Anger burned in Cole's hazel stare as he nodded. ''Sweetheart, I wouldn't trust him any farther than I could pick the bastard up and throw him.''

She stared at Cole for several long seconds. He was too close for her to ignore how sexy he was, or how handsome.

''For your information, my training at the academy in Quantico covers most of your concerns,'' she said, finally finding her voice. ''But let me give you a rundown, in order to put your mind at ease, Caveman. I've been trained in both psychological and physical defensive tactics, as well as marksmanship. I was at the top of my class, and I think I can handle Valente just as well as you can.''

When she started to walk away, Cole caught her by the shoulder. ''It doesn't hurt to have a little insurance, sweetheart.''

She stepped back. ''I do appreciate your concern,

Caveman. But I can take care of myself. I don't need a pretend lover to protect me.''

His anger and frustration close to the boiling point, Cole watched Campbell disappear through the entrance to the inn. This was what he got for trying to be a gentleman and protect the woman from the dangers she was too hardheaded to see for herself.

Shaking his head, he got back in the SUV and spun gravel as he pulled out of the parking lot and onto the road. Not only did he need to cool off, he needed to make arrangements to get her rental car back to the inn.

As he drove through town, he thought about how he was going to juggle following his leads, while protecting her at the same time. What he should do is just back off, conduct his own investigation and let her find out for herself just how devious Valente really was.

But even as the thought was forming, Cole shook his head. That would be like throwing a lamb to the wolves. And whether he liked it or not, that was something he just couldn't do.

Whether Special Agent Campbell of the FBI liked it or not, for all intents and purposes, ATF Special Agent Cole Yardley was her boyfriend for as long as they were in Mission Creek conducting their investigations of Ricky Mercado and the infamous Mercado crime family.

The next morning, Elise sat in the lobby of the Mission Creek First Federal Bank, waiting to present the new bank president with a court order seizing the banking records of the late Carmine Mercado and the late Frank Del Brio. As soon as she concluded her business here, she'd serve a similar document on the very much alive Ricky Mercado. Once she'd collected everything, she'd go back to the inn and spend the rest of the day comparing figures to the Mercado trucking and produce business accounts. And if there was even a hint of a link between them, she'd find it.

Checking her watch, she wondered what could possibly be taking the bank president so long. It had been a good half hour since one of the tellers had informed him that she was waiting to see him.

Just as Elise was about to get up to ask the woman to remind the man that she was waiting, the door to his office opened and out strolled Caveman Cole. She could have bitten nails in two. What was he doing here? His investigation certainly didn't include reviewing financial records.

As he walked up to her, her pulse fluttered. Now why on earth had that happened? And why was his smile so…friendly? But more importantly, why was she smiling back?

"Good morning, Elise," he said pleasantly. "I see you found your car."

She nodded cautiously. What was he up to this time? He'd used her first name. He'd never done that before. "I assume you were responsible for seeing that it was returned to the inn last night?"

He grinned and her temperature rose a good ten degrees. "I figured you'd need it today."

"Agent Campbell, Mr. Harling will see you now," the teller said, standing beside the open office door.

"I'll be right there," she told the woman. Thankful to be escaping Yardley's disturbing presence, she turned to him. "Thank you for returning the car. Now if you'll excuse me, I have a meeting."

"See you later, sweetheart." His voice seemed to echo throughout the bank lobby.

When several bank patrons turned to look their way, Elise felt as if her cheeks were on fire. "Why on earth did you say that?" she asked, lowering her voice so only he could hear. "Now these people think there's something going on between us."

Nodding, he grinned. "That's the plan."

"Why?" Shocked beyond belief, she couldn't seem to do anything but stand and gape at him.

He leaned close to whisper in her ear. "Remember, I told you that your every move is being watched. That's one of Valente's men standing over by the new-accounts window."

Elise looked around, but the only man she saw, other than the bank guard, was a little old man of about seventy leaning on his cane. "Yeah, right, Yardley." Fuming, she shook her head. "I don't have time for your silly little games. I'm late for my meeting. But this isn't over. As soon as I have the time, I'm going to set you straight on a few things, Caveman."

Grinning, he turned and headed for the door. "I'll be looking forward to it, sweetheart."

Cole stood, propped against the fender of Elise's car as he waited for her to come out of the bank. He had no doubt that the first chance she got, she'd give him a tongue-lashing for that little scene in the lobby. But that couldn't be helped. The sooner that word got around about them being together, the safer she'd be from Valente's tactics.

Not that he thought she'd fall for one of Valente's lines. Elise had a lot more intelligence than that. It was John Valente's persistence that bothered him. The man wasn't used to having people tell him no. Coupled with Valente's complete lack of scruples, and Cole had a feeling that the man embodied the kind of trouble he didn't even want to think about.

No, it was much safer to listen to her call him a caveman and read him the riot act every chance she got than to let her take her chances with a viper like Valente.

Once Elise collected all the records she needed for her investigation, and she was safely tucked away in her room at the Mission Creek Inn crunching numbers, Cole would resume his investigation and solve the case.

He smiled when he looked up and saw her shouldering her way through the bank's tempered-glass doors with a big file box. "Need some help, Campbell?"

"I can manage."

He watched her struggle for a moment before stepping forward to take the box from her. "Where do you want it? The trunk or the back seat?"

"Trunk," she answered, pushing the button on the remote to release the latch.

When he placed the heavy box inside, then slammed it shut, he looked up to find her glaring at him. "What?"

"Why were you waiting for me?"

He smiled. "You're welcome."

"Oh…yes, thank you." She frowned. "Don't change the subject."

Shrugging, he walked around to the passenger side of her car and opened the door. "I thought I'd ride out to Ricky Mercado's place with you."

Her vivid emerald gaze narrowed as she stared at him across the top of the car. "How did you know that's where I'm going next?"

"I talked to Sheriff Wainwright yesterday when he helped me get your car back to the inn." Cole lowered himself into the passenger seat at the same time she opened the driver's door. He wasn't giving her the chance to leave without him. "I told him I'd ride along with you when you go to serve Mercado with the court order for his financial records."

She slid in behind the wheel, then turned to stare at him. "Let me get this straight. You decided all of this for me, without even asking if I was agreeable. Is that correct?"

"Well, it wasn't exactly like that," he said, buckling the shoulder harness.

"Then why don't you tell me *exactly* how it was?" Her eyes sparkled with anger, fascinating the hell out of him.

Cole shrugged. "Wainwright mentioned that he had to make a trip up to Austin after he accompanied you out to Mercado's and I volunteered to take his place."

"And why would you do that?" she demanded, brushing a stray lock of hair from her forehead. "Why aren't you running down your own leads?"

He had to fight the urge to reach out and run his

fingers through her auburn curls. "I am following a lead. Ricky Mercado is my prime suspect."

She shook her head, surprising him. "I think you're wrong."

"What makes you think he's not involved?"

"For all I know, he may be involved to some degree," she said, starting the car. "But I don't think he's the mastermind of the operation."

"The gun smuggling didn't start until after Mercado came back from Mezcaya." Had she already discovered something in Valente's accounts to indicate otherwise?

"That's true. The smuggling wasn't discovered until after he returned. But I have a feeling it was set up to look that way."

"Women's intuition, huh?" he asked, laughing out loud. Instead of insisting that he get out of the car, she pulled from the parking space. Apparently, she'd been distracted by arguing with him about the case.

Her expression anything but amused, she glanced over at him. "Never underestimate the accuracy of a woman's instincts, Caveman."

"I'll try to remember that while putting the cuffs on Mercado and reading him his rights, *sweetheart*."

Four

At the sound of a car slowing down on the main road, Ricky Mercado looked up from the board he'd been measuring. What now? he wondered, watching the red sedan kick up the dry south Texas dust as it started down the lane leading to his new home. He couldn't tell who was in the car, only that it had two passengers.

He shook his head. It had to be more of those damn government agents, coming to harass him. They were the only visitors he seemed to have these days. Most of his friends were either too busy enjoying their first few months of wedded bliss, or avoiding him because they'd heard he was being investigated by the feds.

Slamming the tape measure on top of the board, he marched down the steps, then folded his arms across his chest as he waited for the car to stop. He was getting sick and tired of answering the same questions over and over, and he had every intention of telling whoever got out of the car that if they couldn't cough up some solid evidence against him, to leave him the hell alone.

But when a tall, slender, auburn-haired woman got out of the driver's side, he grinned. Maybe his luck was changing for the better. Whatever agency she was from, it sure as hell had better-looking operatives than the ATF.

"Mr. Mercado?" She held up a leather-encased badge. "I'm Special Agent Elise Campbell with the FBI."

"What can I do for you today, Agent Campbell?" Smiling, he gazed at the attractive woman walking toward him. She had a set of legs on her that wouldn't quit, and that slim black skirt emphasized how slender and shapely she was.

He appeared to focus his full attention on her, but years of military training and a lifetime of being a Mercado had taught him to always be aware of what was going on around him. It was what had kept him alive for thirty-five years. That's why he knew immediately when the passenger inside the sedan moved to open the door. Ricky tensed, ready to take whatever defensive action was needed, until he realized it was Yardley stepping out of the car.

Nodding his acknowledgment of the man, Ricky never took his eyes off the woman in front of him. "Yardley."

The ATF agent walked up to stand beside the Campbell woman. "Anything changed in the past couple of days, Mercado?"

"Nope. Anything new with you?"

Yardley tucked his hands in the back pockets of his jeans as he glanced over at the woman, then shook his head. "Same old, same old."

Ricky studied the man who had harassed him nearly every day for the past week with questions about being in Mezcaya and the gun-smuggling ring operating in Mission Creek. But there was a tension about Yardley today that Ricky hadn't seen before. His stance, the way he kept glancing from the very pretty Agent Campbell to Ricky, spoke volumes. Unless he missed his guess, Yardley had the hots for the FBI chick.

"Mr. Mercado—"

"Call me Ricky," he said, giving her his most charming smile. From the corner of his eye, he watched Yardley frown.

Yep. He'd been right. Yardley had it bad and probably didn't even realize it. Oh, he was going to have fun with this. *Payback time, brother.*

"Agent Campbell, whatever you need, just ask." He purposely turned up the wattage on his smile. "Would you like to go inside where it's cooler?"

"No, thank you, Mr.—"

"The name's Ricky," he said, lowering his voice to add intimacy.

She nodded. "All right…Ricky. I'm sorry, but this isn't a social call."

"That's a shame." He almost laughed out loud when Yardley's frown turned to a deep scowl. "To what do I owe the pleasure of your visit, Agent Campbell?"

Her smile was almost apologetic as she handed him

a paper. "This is a court order freezing your assets and requiring you to turn over all of your financial records for the purpose of an ongoing investigation."

Anger burned at Ricky's gut. Why couldn't the feds get it through their thick skulls that he wasn't involved with the Mercado crime family any longer? Why couldn't they accept that he'd stopped living his life on the other side of legal, and gone straight?

But to the attractive woman in front of him, he gave what he hoped was an understanding smile and nodded. "I'll be more than happy to cooperate in any way I can."

"Thank you, Ricky." She looked relieved, and he'd bet every dime he had that she wasn't sent to work cases out of the office very often. "I really appreciate your willingness to make my job easier."

"It's my pleasure," Ricky lied. He thought he heard the man beside her mutter an oath. "What was that, Yardley?"

Yardley rocked back on his heels and shook his head. "I didn't say anything."

Placing his hand at Agent Campbell's back, Ricky smiled down at her. "Why don't we go inside and you can take whatever you need for your investigation."

As they ascended the steps and walked across the porch, he wasn't at all surprised to hear Yardley close on their heels. The man wasn't going to let the very attractive FBI agent out of his sight.

The only consolation Ricky found in the otherwise intolerable situation was the knowledge that he was frustrating the hell out of Yardley—first by turning on the charm with a lady that Yardley had the hots for, then showing a willingness to cooperate with her that Ricky had never shown him.

If circumstances had been different, he might have laughed out loud. But there was nothing funny about this latest turn of events. They were focusing too much attention on him, and not looking for the real perpetrator of the gun-smuggling ring. And he was damn tired of waiting around for them to figure it out.

It was time to take some action. As soon as Yardley and his FBI chick left, Ricky had every intention of doing some investigating on his own.

Elise looked around the dining room of the Mission Creek Inn as she waited for the kindhearted innkeeper, Mrs. Carter, to seat her. She wouldn't have bothered coming down for dinner, but the last six hours had taken their toll and she needed a break. From the time she'd returned to the inn around noon, she'd holed up in her room, going over pages and pages of computer printouts and adding endless columns of figures on balance sheets.

"Honey, you look like you could use some good old-fashioned home cookin'," Mrs. Carter said, motioning for Elise to follow. "How does a chicken-fried steak, red-eye gravy, a big old heap of mashed potatoes and some sourdough bread with homemade butter sound?"

"Fattening," Elise murmured. To the grandmotherly Mrs. Carter, she said, "I'm really not that hungry."

"Nonsense," the woman said, pointing to a table with a red-checkered tablecloth. "You have a seat there and I'll fix you right up."

Elise started to protest that she'd prefer a salad, but one look at the woman's face and she knew it would be pointless to argue. Some women were just the mothering type. Mrs. Carter was one of them.

Resigned to having to run an extra mile the next morning in order to work off the extra calories, she nodded. "That will be fine, Mrs. Carter."

Apparently satisfied that she'd get to feed Elise, Mrs. Carter started to walk toward the kitchen, then turned back. "I hope you don't mind, but I'm going to have to seat another guest at your table this evening."

Looking around, Elise frowned. There were ten tables in the tiny dining room and only three were being used. "No, I don't mind, Mrs. Carter. But—"

"Oh, there's your dinner partner now," Mrs. Carter said, bustling off toward the entrance. When she returned, the woman had Caveman Cole in tow. "I think you've met Miss Campbell, haven't you, Mr. Yardley?"

"Yes, ma'am," Cole answered, looking as confused as Elise felt. "We're acquainted."

"Wonderful." Mrs. Carter pointed to the empty chair. "You have a seat and I'll be back in just a minute with your meal."

As the woman hurried off to the kitchen, Cole looked even more confused. "But I haven't ordered yet."

Elise shook her head as Cole seated himself across from her. "Don't bother. I tried to tell her that I'd like a salad, but she's bringing me a fried steak, mashed potatoes and gravy. And I suspect you'll get the same."

His deep chuckle sent a tremor coursing through her. "Did you ask her to seat me at your table?"

"Hardly." Taking a sip of water, she tried to ignore the sudden quickening of her pulse as his knees bumped hers beneath the small table. "Did you ask to sit with me?"

He shook his head. "I think—"

"We're being set up."

Grinning, he nodded. "I do believe dear Mrs. Carter has a romantic streak."

"Oh, great. She's not only trying to fatten me up, she's trying to fix me up."

"And with a caveman, no less," he added, his charming expression curling her toes.

"Well, I do suppose it could be worse," she said, unable to stop her own smile.

"Sure it could. I could be a caveman with lousy table manners." His grin widened as he held out his hands for her inspection. "But, as you can see, my hands are clean. I only dragged my knuckles a couple of times on the way down here for dinner."

Elise stared at his large hands. They were strong-looking and masculine, with a light sprinkling of dark hair across the backs. How would they feel caressing her bare skin? Touching her as he—

Shocked by her wayward thoughts, she reached for her water glass and took a sip to keep from coughing. Caveman Cole was the very last man she was interested in. He was not only a fellow federal agent, he also had an attitude toward women that she found completely intolerable. But as she stared at him across the rim of her glass, she had to admit that she'd learned something about him in the last couple of days that she hadn't realized before. Cole Yardley's caveman tendencies didn't stem from a male-superiority complex as she'd first thought. She suspected his opinion concerning female agents not belonging in the field was due to a protectiveness he felt toward women, not because he viewed them as inferior.

"Here you go, kids," Mrs. Carter said, setting two heaping plates of delicious-smelling food in front of them. "I'll be right back with your loaf of bread, a crock of sweet butter and two glasses of iced tea."

Thankful that Mrs. Carter had interrupted her disturbing revelation about Cole Yardley, Elise inhaled the rich aroma rising from her plate. "It smells wonderful."

"Is this the first time you've had Mrs. Carter's cooking?" Cole asked.

Nodding, she placed her red linen napkin in her lap. "Last night I grabbed a package of cheese crackers and a bottle of mineral water and stayed in my room going over the Mercado Trucking accounts. And the night before that, I picked up a pepperoni pizza to bring back to my room. Remember, you helped yourself to some of it."

He sliced into the steak with his knife. "That's right. It was just before we butted heads."

"We seem to do that a lot."

Looking up, he grinned. "Until the other night, it had only been figuratively."

As they ate the scrumptious food, they talked about his lack of siblings and her two older sisters; his being raised by a single Marine Corps father and her being raised by a single, independent mother.

"What happened to your dad?" Cole asked as he polished off the last bite of his steak.

"He was killed in a car accident when I was six months old." She smiled sadly. "All I've ever really had are pictures of him and stories that my mother shared. I always wanted a father, but my mother never remarried. She said that he was the love of her life and she refused to settle for less."

Cole nodded. "That sounds like my dad. Gunny met my mom the summer he finished boot camp. He always said that he took one look and knew that she was the one. They married two weeks later."

"They didn't know each other very long," Elise said, wondering how anyone could be sure of something that important so soon after meeting.

"You'd have to know my dad." Cole chuckled. "Once Gunny decided on something, that was the way it was."

"Why do you call him Gunny?"

"He was Marine Corps through and through and that's what he preferred. Gunny always said there were two loves in his life—my mom and the corps." Looking wistful, Cole leaned back in his chair. "After Mom died, Gunny devoted himself to raising me and going wherever the corps sent him."

"How old were you when—"

"My mom died?" When she nodded, he stared off into space as if trying to remember the woman who had given him life. "I had just turned four. Gunny had received orders to go overseas, so he sent my mom and me to stay with my grandparents on their ranch in Nevada. Mom was helping my grandmother store some things in the attic and fell off a ladder.

She was about two months pregnant at the time. As soon as she started hemorrhaging, my grandparents started for the hospital with her, but the ranch was so far from the nearest town with a doctor, they couldn't get her there in time. She died on the way.''

Elise reached out to cover his hand where it rested on top of the table. "I'm so sorry, Cole. That must have been very hard on you and your father.''

"It wasn't the best of times," he said, shaking his head solemnly. "But having to move every year or so, we had to rely on each other for so much, we worked it out.''

She could tell it hadn't been as easy on him as Cole tried to let on. She gave his hand a gentle squeeze "I can't imagine not living in the same house all of my life. It must have been upsetting to get settled in somewhere, then have to move again.''

"It was pretty tough for a while. Just when I'd start to make friends, Gunny would get orders to move on to another base.'' Shrugging, he gave her a noncommittal look. "I finally gave up trying to get acquainted with other kids and occupied myself with learning all about guns and explosives.''

"Oh, that's a wonderful hobby for a child," she said dryly. "Very safe.''

"At least I didn't blow up anything." He grinned. "Unless you count the time I made my own fireworks and blew our mailbox off the post, trying to test a homemade cherry bomb.''

"You didn't.''

"Sure did." He laughed. "You should have seen it. I put the device inside the mailbox, and when it went off, the damn thing flew a good twenty feet in the air, the flag spun around a couple of times and the flap fell off.''

Elise laughed so hard she had to wipe tears from her eyes. ''What did your dad say? Was he upset about the mailbox?''

''Gunny was helping me test it,'' Cole said, laughing and shaking his head. ''After it landed, he walked over to see what was left, then looked back at me and asked, 'Think you used a little too much gunpowder in that one, son?' ''

As their laughter subsided, the feel of his warm palm caressing hers, and the sound of his deep laughter had heat spreading throughout her entire body. When they worked the El Paso case two years ago, why hadn't she noticed how nice his smile was, or how funny he could be?

As she sat trying to sort out the Cole she'd thought she knew from the man sitting across the table from her, he absently began to trace lazy circles over her wrist with his thumb. Her pulse skipped a beat and a shiver coursed through her. And that wasn't good. Not at all.

This was Cole Yardley, ATF maverick, and the last man she should be shivering over. Even if they hadn't irritated each other from the moment they met, her golden rule about dating other federal agents would prevent her from seeing him.

Slowly extricating her hand from his, she made a point of glancing at her watch. ''I hate to cut this short, but if I intend to get a couple more hours of auditing done tonight, I'd better go back to work.'' Good heavens, had that breathless voice really been hers?

He checked his own watch, then nodded and rose from his chair. "I need to get going, too."

"You kids have a nice evening," Mrs. Carter called from the kitchen door. "I'll see you for breakfast in the morning. We start serving at six."

"Thank you," Elise said, turning to smile at the older woman. "But I'll probably just call and have some coffee sent to my room."

Turning back toward the exit, she started to bid Cole a good evening, but he was nowhere in sight.

Cole sat in the SUV on a road several hundred yards from the back of Ricky Mercado's place, looking through a pair of night-vision binoculars. In the past two hours, he'd watched the man replace the boards on his back steps, down a couple of beers and cuss a raccoon every time the animal poked its head out from beneath the porch. But there had been no signs of suspicious activity, and nothing to indicate that Mercado was anything more than what he appeared to be—a regular guy working to renovate his house.

Lowering the field glasses, Cole rubbed his eyes. He hated surveillance. It had to be the most boring part of his job. But if he got the lead he was looking for, it would be well worth the long hours of sitting in the cramped confines of the truck. The sooner he got the goods on Mercado, the sooner he could go back to Vegas and forget about the woman who had him so tied up in knots he didn't know which end was up anymore.

It started with that kiss in the country-club parking lot and it hadn't stopped since. Every time he was around her, he had to fight the urge to touch her, to pull her into his arms and kiss her again.

But what really had him questioning his own sanity was his reaction to the interest Mercado had shown Elise this morning when she'd served him with the court order. Ricky Mercado had turned the charm on so thick with Elise that Cole had damn near choked on it. And that bothered him. A lot.

The ruse he had created that he and Elise were more than just co-workers was exactly that—a farce. Cole had no interest in the woman beyond keeping her safe from that snake Valente. Did he?

Cursing, he picked up the binoculars and once again trained them on the house. He didn't want to think about how charming she'd been at dinner this evening, or how her laughter and the softness of her skin had made him want to do more than just kiss her.

Movement at the back of the house had him straightening in his seat as he watched Mercado go inside and shut the door. Watching closely for the next thirty minutes, Cole could tell that the man was calling it a night. With no curtains on the windows, he could easily see Mercado move from room to room, turning off lights downstairs. When he entered one of the rooms upstairs, then shut off the light, Cole figured Mercado had gone to bed.

But that didn't mean it wasn't a show to divert the attention of anyone who might be watching. Mercado could still leave, or meet with someone at the house under the cover of darkness.

Cole decided to give it a couple more hours before he went back to the inn. He had a feeling that he'd spend a sleepless night anyway just knowing that Elise was in the next room, lying in bed, probably dressed in something sexy as hell.

His groin tightened, causing him to cuss a blue streak. He wasn't the least bit attracted to Elise. He just wished like hell his body would remember that fact.

Elise spoke to the night clerk at the desk as she walked through the lobby on her way to the inn's courtyard. It was almost midnight and she'd spent all evening comparing the accounts of the deceased heads of the mob and Ricky Mercado's records to the Mercado Trucking and the Superior Produce Company books. She needed a breath of fresh air to clear her mind before she turned in for the night.

The moon and stars lit her way and she had no trouble following the winding paths through the well-kept beds of cactus and native Texas wildflowers. When she reached the back of the garden, she climbed the steps of a gazebo and sat down on the wooden swing suspended by chains from the center rafter.

As she sat enjoying the faint scent of bougainvillea drifting on the cooler night air, she wondered where Cole had gone for the evening. She hadn't seen or heard from him since he disappeared so mysteriously from the inn's dining room earlier in the evening.

"What the hell do you think you're doing out here at this time of night by yourself?"

Elise jumped at the unexpected sound of Cole's angry voice. "Good heavens, you just frightened me half to death," she said, placing her hand to her chest.

"You should be afraid," he said, sounding angry.

He walked up the steps and over to sit beside her on the swing. "You have no business being out here at night by yourself."

"You're kidding, right?"

"No, I'm not." The moonlight filtering through the open sides of the gazebo shed enough light for her to see his stormy expression, and she had no doubt he meant everything he said. "What if Valente or one of his henchmen saw you out here alone?"

"What if they did? There's a fence around this garden." She shook her head. "There isn't even a way to get in here without going through the inn's lobby."

Cole snorted. "Hellfire, woman, the picket fence around this little pea patch isn't more than four feet high. Don't you think someone could climb the damn thing?"

"It's not a pea patch. It's a flower and cactus garden," she corrected.

"Whatever," he muttered.

"And why would anyone climb the fence when the garden is open to anyone?"

He made a sound that sounded suspiciously like a growl. "For an FBI agent, you are without a doubt the most naive woman I've ever encountered. What if Valente wanted to kidnap you? Or worse?"

"Why would he do that? You said yourself he turned over a doctored set of the trucking and produce company books," Elise argued. "He's quite confident that I won't find anything to link him or his companies to the gun smuggling."

"Have you ever heard of a criminal insuring that nothing is found?" He shook his head. "From now on, if you want to go traipsing around outside your room after midnight, let me know. I'll take you for a walk.''

''Oh, really. You'll *take* me for a walk like an obedient pet?''

''Okay, so I'll accompany you.'' His voice sounded a little less angry.

''Let me clue you in on something, *Caveman.*'' So angry that she found it impossible to sit still, Elise rose to her feet. ''I'll go where I want, when I want, and without you. Is that clear?''

He stood up to face her. ''Not if it's pitch-black dark you won't, *sweetheart.*''

''Yes, I will.''

''No, you won't.''

''Watch me.'' She started to march down the steps of the gazebo, but he caught her by the arm.

''Elise, listen to me.''

Cole's tone of voice was almost urgent, and he'd used her name. She could have easily resisted turning back if he hadn't done that. But his deep baritone saying her name sent a shiver straight through her, and she could no more stop herself from facing him than she could pluck the stars from the sky.

''What?''

He started to say something, then shook his head and pulled her into his arms. Before she could react, his mouth came down on hers as he crushed her to him, and the heady feeling of his lips once again pressed to hers took her breath.

Every cell in her body tingled to life as he coaxed, demanded and persuaded her to respond, and Elise found herself opening for him, urging him to deepen the kiss. She might have been shocked by her reaction, but rational thought was beyond her capabilities. Cole's firm lips moving over hers, the tip of his tongue seeking entry, left her with nothing but the ability to feel.

Hunger, swift and hot, swirled through her and she curled her fingers in his soft, knit T-shirt to keep from melting into a puddle at his big, booted feet. The rock-hard muscles of his chest quivered beneath her hands and an answering tremor coursed through her. But when his tongue invaded the inner recesses of her mouth, the taste of his desire, the heady sensation of his tender stroking, sent a warm current flowing through her and caused her knees to give way.

When she sagged against him, he caught and held her close, allowing her to feel the firm insistence of his arousal as he shamelessly pressed himself into her lower belly. His breathing harsh, he broke the kiss, then leaned back to look down at her. The need, the burning passion she saw in his hazel eyes sent a shiver of delight straight to the most feminine part of her.

He stared at her for endless seconds before bringing his hands up to tangle his fingers in her hair. "When I found you missing from your room..." His voice trailed off as if he was unable or unwilling to put into words what he'd felt. Taking a deep breath, he shook his head. "Please, promise me you won't go out at night like this again, unless I'm with you."

If she'd been able to form words, she'd have told him that she'd do no such thing. But even as her mind resisted his ridiculous request, she nodded her agreement.

* * *

Cole glanced at the clock on the beside table, then forcefully punched his pillow. It would be getting light soon, but he hadn't so much as closed his eyes. Every time he did, he remembered the cold emptiness that had gripped him when he'd opened the door between his and Elise's room, only to find she wasn't there. In that split second when he'd realized she was gone, a thousand different scenarios had run through his mind, and all of them had ended with her fighting off John Valente's slimy touch.

Throwing the sheet back, he swung his legs over the side of the bed, sat up, and propping his arms on his knees, rested his head in his hands. What the hell was wrong with him? And what had possessed him to grab her and kiss her until they both came close to collapsing from lack of oxygen?

Why was he feeling this way about her? She was nothing like the calm, agreeable women he was normally attracted to. Elise Campbell had an acerbic tongue, an argumentative streak that drove him nuts, and her stubbornness would drive Job over the edge.

Sighing, he stood and walked into the bathroom to splash cold water on his face. He didn't need this. He worked alone. And that's the way he liked it.

But the thought of Valente laying a hand on her, whether from anger or lust, caused Cole to grit his teeth against the pure fury burning at his gut. Why was he so consumed with the need to protect her from Valente?

He'd tried telling himself that she was too inexperienced in fieldwork to know how to deal with the head of the Mercado crime family, and that all he wanted to do was make sure she didn't get into something she couldn't deal with. But there were other, more intelligent, ways he could go about it than grabbing her and kissing her senseless whenever he got the chance.

Hell, it was no wonder she insisted on calling him Caveman. The only thing he hadn't done was throw her over his shoulder to drag her back to his bed. And he'd even mentioned doing that to her.

He shook his head, walked back to the bed and stretched out. Staring at the ceiling, he blew out a frustrated breath. In the past three days, he'd displayed less smarts than that of a day-old jackass.

But the memory of Elise's sweet lips beneath his, the feel of her soft body pressed to his, had him feeling more protective, more territorial than he'd ever felt in his life. And he had the disturbing suspicion that until this case was brought to a close, that emotion was only going to intensify.

Five

Elise yawned as she tried to concentrate on the columns of figures in front of her. She'd been trying for the past hour to find a discrepancy between Carmine Mercado's accounts, those of his successor, Frank Del Brio, and the records of the Mercado Trucking Company. On the surface, everything looked to be in order, but even though the numbers added up, there was something that bothered her. She couldn't put her finger on it just yet, but she knew whatever it was, she'd find it.

Giving up for the moment, she leaned back in the chair and rubbed her eyes. Part of the reason she was having trouble concentrating was due to her run-in with Cole last night in the inn's courtyard. The memory of his kiss, the way she'd clung to him, caused her cheeks to burn and a languorous heat to flow throughout her body.

Had she lost her mind? How could she be heating up over a man she didn't even like. And how could she have ignored her hard, fast rule of not fraternizing with anyone she worked with?

But as she thought of Cole holding her, kissing her like she'd never been kissed before, her lips tingled and her stomach fluttered as if a flock of butterflies had been released inside.

Finding it hard to sit still, she pushed away from the desk, stood up and walked over to stare out the window at the inn's garden below. The pretty, white gazebo at the back of the courtyard was hidden from view by the canopy of live oak trees surrounding it.

Why Caveman Cole? What was there about him that she suddenly found so...tempting?

He was the same overbearing man he'd been two years ago. Wasn't he? She nodded. Of course he was. Why was she even doubting it? And why was she finding it so hard to forget about him—his smile, the deep, rich sound of his laughter and the feel of his firm male lips on hers?

A delicious tension suddenly gripped her body, and her knees didn't want to support her. Walking back over to the desk, she marked her place on the print-outs, jotted down the figure on the calculator screen, then shut it off. Some things were better left unexplored and her sudden attraction to Caveman Cole Yardley was one of them. What she needed was something to get her mind off the man and back to the business of finding the paper trail she was sure connected the Mercado family to the gun smuggling ring.

Glancing at her watch, she walked over to the bureau to pull out a hot-pink spandex sports bra and matching shorts. She shoved them into a canvas gym bag, then as an afterthought added her swimsuit and a clean change of clothes. She'd work off the unwarranted tension in the Lone Star's fitness room, then swim a few laps in the indoor Olympic pool for good measure. By the time she finished, she'd be relaxed and ready to get back to finding the link between the guns being funneled to the El Jefé terrorists in Mezcaya and the Mercado crime family.

She smiled as she grabbed her car keys and headed for the door. With the entire town shutting down for the weekend, and converging on the club for its annual summer festival, she was sure Ricky Mercado and John Valente would be present. She might have the opportunity to observe them doing something that led to a break in her investigation.

And the sooner that happened, the sooner she could go back to Virginia and distance herself from Cole Yardley. Maybe then she'd regain her good sense.

The huge indoor swimming area was relatively deserted when Elise finished her workout and changed into her two-piece swimsuit. Most everyone was outside on the country club's patio and lawn enjoying the outdoor-barbecue buffet, and choosing their partner for the relay games that would follow immediately after lunch.

A young couple passed her on their way out, leaving her alone with a man swimming laps in the huge pool. As he neared the end where she stood, she found herself staring at the way the corded muscles in his arms and back bunched and flexed with each stroke.

The man had a very impressive physique and she could tell he was in the habit of working out regularly. When he reached the side and did a perfect underwater turn, his powerful legs pushed off the side of the pool, propelling him through the water much like a torpedo, and well into his next lap. Having been on the swim team all through high school, she recognized the smooth way he sliced through the water with a minimum of disturbance as the moves of a very experienced swimmer.

But there was something about the man that was familiar, something that made every nerve in her body tingle to full alert. As he reached the near end of the pool, and she got a glimpse of his face, it suddenly dawned on her why. Caveman Cole was the man performing the strokes so expertly.

Great! She'd come to the country club to try to avoid thinking about him, and here she stood, tingling over his fantastic body.

Deciding to leave before he realized she'd been watching him, Elise cringed when he reached the opposite side of the pool, then, stopping to hold on to the side, called her name. "Hey, Campbell. Want to race?"

She shook her head. "No."

"Think I could beat you, huh?"

"Not in this lifetime," she said, laughing.

He leisurely swam over to the side where she stood. "Then what's stopping you from showing me?"

"I don't want to damage your fragile male ego, Caveman."

He laughed. "Sounds like you know you can't win and you're using that as an excuse."

She shook her head. "It looks like I'm going to have to show you," she said, reaching for the sarong wrapped around her waist. "Just remember, I tried to save your ego the crushing blow of being beaten by a woman."

As she unwound the long gauzy cloth from her trim waist, Cole tried his damnedest not to stare. The two-piece suit was modest compared to most bikinis, but on Elise it couldn't have looked more provocative. He tried to concentrate on how the deep, jewel-blue suit contrasted with her auburn hair. But it was the way the top cupped her full breasts and the bottoms clung to her shapely hips that had him feeling as if he might never take another breath.

When she tossed the wrap on a lounge then walked to the edge of the pool, he gulped. Her long, slender legs were perfect for wrapping around a man and holding him to her as she drained every ounce of energy from him. His body responded and he was extremely glad that he was already in the pool.

Diving neatly into the water, she surfaced beside him, and he wondered what he'd been thinking when he'd goaded her into this race. How the hell was he going to be able to swim, let alone win, in his condition?

"Are you ready?" she asked, smiling as if she knew something he didn't.

Stalling, he shook his head as he tried to bring his body back under control. "We haven't decided on the number of laps, or what the winner gets."

"How about two laps?" she asked.

"Think that's all you can do?"

"You wish!" Her delighted laughter echoed

throughout the pool area. "I was just trying to take pity on you since you've been swimming for a while."

Cole grinned. "Don't worry about me, sweetheart. I can hold my own. Let's go four laps."

"So what do I win when I beat you, Caveman?"

"I'll buy your dinner for the next week."

"And if you win?"

He reached out to wipe a droplet of water running down her cheek. "I haven't decided yet."

Her easy expression disappeared. "I don't think I like not knowing—"

"Ready, set, go!"

He took off before Elise could protest his noncommittal answer. In the unlikely event that she beat him, he figured he'd go easy on her and let her buy him a beer. But she didn't know that and he wasn't about to tell her.

When he made the first turn at the opposite end of the pool, he wasn't at all surprised that she was right behind him. He'd slowed his normal pace in order to let her think she at least had a chance of winning. But by the time he'd completed three laps and started on the last leg of their race, it came as no small surprise that she was right with him. She was a stronger swimmer than he'd anticipated.

She pulled ahead and he found himself having to draw on his reserves to catch up. Just as they reached the side of the pool, he gave it all he had, but she managed to touch the edge a split second before he did.

"You've done...this before," he said, trying to catch his breath.

Nodding, she wiped the water from her eyes and grinned. "I was on the swim team all four years in high school, and state champion in my senior year."

"You tried to hustle me."

"No, I didn't," she said, shaking her head. "You were the one who challenged me."

"Yes, but you failed to tell me about swimming competitively."

She shrugged. "Get over it, Yardley. I won fair and square."

When she started to haul herself up on the side of the pool, he stopped her by putting a hand on her shoulder. "But I would have won if I hadn't gone easy on you." At the feel of her wet skin beneath his palm, it suddenly didn't matter who won. Wrapping one arm around her waist, he pulled her close.

"Wh-what do you...think you're doing?" she asked, sounding more breathless than she had right after completing their race.

He smiled. "I'm collecting the consolation prize."

"This isn't smart, Yardley."

"Probably not. But then, we cavemen aren't know for being overly intelligent." Before she could protest further, he lowered his head and captured her mouth with his.

The water lapped at their chins and, careful to hold them above the surface, Cole leisurely savored her lips as he reacquainted himself with their softness. When Elise brought her arms up to circle his neck, he pulled her more fully against him and the feel of her bare abdomen and lush breasts pressed to his chest sent a shock wave straight to the most sensitive part of his anatomy.

When she sighed at the contact, he instinctively knew she was experiencing the same intense sensation he was. Taking advantage of her acceptance, he slipped inside to taste the sweetness that was uniquely Elise. Boldly stroking her tongue with his, he teased her into a game of advance and retreat, then coaxed her into exploring him as he'd explored her. The tension between them rapidly increased and when she brought her legs up to wrap around his waist, it felt as if the blood in his veins turned to liquid fire.

Her smooth thighs held him captive as she tentatively acquainted herself with him, and it was all Cole could do to keep them afloat. Never in his life had his arousal been so swift or as intense as it was at that very moment.

Deciding that they'd both end up drowning if he didn't put a halt to things, and damn quick, Cole broke the kiss. "Damn, sweetheart, remind me to make bets with you more often."

No sooner had the words left his mouth than he wished he could call them back. The passion in her emerald eyes faded instantly and she unwrapped her legs from around his waist as she tried to put distance between them.

"I...I need to—" She stopped as if searching for something that needed her immediate attention. "...get back to work."

With his arm still wrapped around her waist, he ignored the signal to release her and shook his head. "Everything in town is closed up tight for the summer festival. There's not a whole lot either of us can do for the rest of the weekend, but maybe watch Mercado's activities here at the Lone Star."

She rested her hands on his shoulders as if she intended to disengage from his embrace. "I have accounts to go over and entries to compare."

Her palms heated his wet skin and made him wonder why steam wasn't rising from where she touched him. He kissed the tip of her cute little nose. "Have you found anything you'd like to share with me?"

Her eyes narrowed a split second before she pushed away from him and hauled herself up onto the side of the pool. "So that's what this was all about. You thought that by kissing me you could gain information about the case I'm building."

How the hell did she get that idea? "No, Elise. I kissed you because—"

"Oh, come on, Yardley." She glared down at him as she grabbed a plush towel. "Do you think I was born yesterday? Your actions speak for themselves. But you're forgetting something."

"What's that?" he asked, fascinated by how gorgeous she was when she was angry.

She shook her head. "We're not sharing information. Or don't you remember your statement that you work alone?"

He watched her vigorously dry herself. The towel skimmed over her creamy skin and touched places he wished his hands were touching. His groin tightened to an almost painful state and he sucked in a sharp breath. What the hell was wrong with him? Elise Campbell didn't even come close to the type of woman he preferred. So why did he want to throw her over his shoulder, take her to a nice secluded place and find out if she was as passionate when she made love as he suspected she'd be.

Cursing under his breath, Cole kicked away from the side of the pool without a backward glance and started swimming laps as fast as his aching muscles would allow. If he swam long enough, maybe he'd be able to forget that kiss, and the fact that he was harder than he'd ever been in his life for a woman who was quickly driving him out of his mind.

When Elise walked into the ladies' locker room, her knees felt as if the cartilage had been replaced with soft rubber. Cole Yardley was the most arrogant, insufferable soul she'd ever encountered. But he kissed like every forbidden fantasy she'd ever had and made her want to forget all about her rule of never becoming involved with a co-worker.

Stripping off her suit, she stepped into the shower, and closing her eyes, stuck her head beneath the spray. She hoped the warm water would wash away all thoughts of the man and how alive he made her feel when he pressed his rigid body to hers. Her lower stomach fluttered and a coil of tension tightened deep inside her feminine regions at the thought of his bare skin touching so much of hers.

"I've lost my mind," she muttered. "That's the only explanation for this insanity."

But twenty minutes later, as she walked out onto the clubhouse patio where the barbecue was being held, her lips still tingled and she couldn't seem to stop the restless feeling deep inside her. "It's just hunger," she muttered.

She'd skipped breakfast and it was well past noon. Like everything else in town, the inn's dining room had closed down for the festivities taking place at the country club. If she didn't eat here, there wasn't much chance of finding something anywhere else.

"It's good to see you again, doll."

At the sound of the gravelly male voice, the skin along the back of Elise's neck prickled and a chill slithered up her spine. Turning, she barely controlled the urge to draw back. "Hello, Mr. Valente."

"Have you eaten yet?" His beady eyes peered at her like those of a rattlesnake watching its prey.

"I was just about to order."

His grin made her feel as if she needed a trip back to the locker room for another shower. "I already have a table. I insist that you join me."

"No, thank you. I have work to do," she said, turning to place her order. She hoped he'd get the message and leave her alone. "Could you make that to go?" she asked the teenager working behind the counter.

When Valente placed his hand at her elbow and jerked her away from the booth, Elise winced. His fingers bit into her skin, and his smile had turned to a deep scowl. "I insist, doll. It's not polite to give someone the bum's rush when he's cooperating with your investigation."

Elise felt a tiny tremor of trepidation skitter through her. Surely he wouldn't try anything in the middle of a crowd. "I told you I don't have time, Mr. Valente," she said firmly. "Now, if you'll excuse me, I'd like to take my food and leave."

"Make that two plates for here," she heard Cole tell the girl behind the counter. Walking over to stand beside her, he nodded an acknowledgment to the man gripping her arm. "Valente."

John Valente looked anything but happy to see Cole. "I was just asking Miss Campbell to join me for lunch, Yardley," he said, loosening his painful grip on her arm.

"I'm afraid you're a bit late. Elise and I arranged to meet here after our swim."

When Cole placed his arm around her shoulders, then leaned down to give her a quick kiss, she didn't even think to protest. John Valente gave her the creeps and no matter what she'd told Cole about her self-defense skills, she wasn't eager to put them to the test in front of the entire town of Mission Creek.

"I'm sorry I kept you waiting, sweetheart. Why don't you go find a table for us while I wait for our lunch."

To Cole's relief, Elise didn't argue and turned to walk across the patio to a group of tables that had been set up on the lawn beneath a live oak tree. "Let me warn you, Valente," he said as he watched her lower herself into one of the patio chairs. "I don't appreciate you bothering my lady." Turning back to the man, pure fury burned deep in Cole's gut at the thought of the mobster's slimy hands on Elise's tender skin. "It better not happen again. Because if it does, you'll find out just what a mean son of a bitch I can be when I'm crossed."

"That goes both ways, Yardley," Valente sneered a moment before he walked away.

Cole watched the crime boss disappear inside the clubhouse. At that moment, nothing would have pleased him more than the pleasure of burying his fist in Valente's ugly face, to prove to the man that he'd meant every word he'd said.

When the teenager working the food booth handed Cole two disposable containers, he turned to find Ricky Mercado sitting across the table from Elise. What the hell was it with the members of the Mercado crime family and their attraction to her? Every time Cole turned around, one of them was trying to hit on her.

"It doesn't appear that he left a mark, Elise," Mercado said as Cole walked up to the table. The fact that the man had used her first name didn't sit well at all, or that he was touching her arm.

"He'd better not have bruised her." Cole placed the containers on the table and sat down beside her to examine her skin. "If he did, I'll leave a few marks on him that time won't fade."

"I'm fine," Elise said, her voice sounding a bit shaky. "He just startled me with his insistence, that's all." Glancing at Mercado, she asked, "Is he like that with everyone?"

Mercado shrugged. "John Valente doesn't like the word *no* from anyone. But especially not from a woman."

"He'd damn well better learn to like it," Cole said, caressing Elise's satiny skin. The thought of anyone leaving a mark on her caused his gut to twist painfully.

"You sound like you know something about Valente that we don't," Elise said.

When Mercado remained silent for several long seconds as if trying to decide how much to tell them, Cole watched the man closely. "It's personal," he finally said, rising to his feet. "Let's just say I've never agreed with Valente's treatment of women and leave it at that.'' He gave Elise a grin that had Cole grinding his teeth. ''But that's something women never have to worry about with me. I know how to treat a lady right.''

With that, Mercado walked across the patio and disappeared into the crowd, leaving Cole so angry that he could taste it.

As he strolled into the Men's Grill to order a beer, Ricky noticed John Valente sitting with a couple of men at a table in one corner of the bar. The fact that John had gotten rough with Agent Campbell didn't surprise Ricky in the least. Valente wasn't known for his tact, or his diplomacy with anyone. But his lack of respect for women was one thing that Ricky had witnessed before, and didn't like one damn bit.

Watching John, Ricky noticed that the two men seated at the table with him were Benito Pascal, the manager of Mercado Trucking, and Mannie Ferrar, the head of Superior Produce. All three of the men were deep in conversation and it was clear that business was being discussed. But instead of looking as if they were displeased, Benito and Mannie both looked quite happy. Which was odd. Ricky knew for a fact that the two older men disliked the new head of the Mercado family immensely.

Part of the problem was that John had never made it a secret about wanting the two old associates to retire. Neither company had ever brought in the kind of big bucks that John Valente was interested in. Carmine hadn't cared how his two old friends had managed the businesses, as long as he got his cut. And Ricky sometimes wondered if Benito and Mannie hung on just to aggravate John, now that he was the head of the family.

So why was Valente so chummy with the two old men now? What did he have going on that he needed to discuss business on a weekend that all of Mission Creek considered a town holiday?

Ricky wasn't sure, but he intended to ask a few questions and find out. It just might be the lead he was looking for that would clear his name with the feds.

Six

Elise moved her food around her plate with a plastic fork in a halfhearted effort to eat the barbecue. She wasn't sure if her lack of appetite was due to her run-in with John Valente, her not having the presence of mind to take defensive action against the man, or because Cole had once again intervened on her behalf.

"I hope you're not worried about Valente," Cole said, taking a swig of his beer. "I don't think he'll be bothering you again."

Apprehension filled her when she glanced up to see a smug look on Cole's handsome face. "Why?"

"Valente and I came to an agreement," he said, sounding quite sure.

Her cheeks heated and anger began to replace her uneasy feeling. Narrowing her eyes, she asked, "What did you say to him?"

Cole shrugged as he gazed off in the distance. "I told him to leave you alone or he'd have me to deal with."

"I can't believe you did that." She shook her head and fought the urge to punch him. "I could have handled the situation on my own. But no, you had to go caveman and rescue the damsel in distress."

"What the hell are you talking about, Elise?" He sounded confused. "I just did what any normal, red-blooded guy would do when some jerk doesn't have the manners of a jackass and starts bothering a woman."

Elise counted to twenty before she trusted herself to explain what was obviously beyond Caveman Cole's comprehension. "Your actions sent John Valente a message all right. It let him know just how incompetent you think I am as a federal agent."

He looked thunderstruck. "How do you figure that?"

"Because instead of giving me the opportunity to assert my authority as a federal agent, you barrel your way into the situation and tell him to leave me alone, like I'm some kind of helpless female." She rose from her chair. "I'm perfectly capable of fighting my own battles, and from now on I'd appreciate it if you'd remember that, Caveman."

She was so angry, she was close to tears as she hurried into the clubhouse to retrieve her gym bag. She fully intended to go back to the inn to finish auditing the records she'd confiscated, find the connection she was sure existed between Mercado Trucking, Superior Produce and the gun-smuggling ring and prove to Cole Yardley just how proficient she was at her job.

But when she walked out of the ladies' locker room, Cole was waiting for her. "Elise, we have to talk."

"No, we don't."

"Dammit, I said we do," he insisted, taking her by the hand.

She allowed him to lead her out onto the huge veranda at the front of the clubhouse. The last thing she wanted to do was to create a scene that would have the good people of Mission Creek talking about the feud between the federal agents investigating the gun smuggling in their fair town.

As soon as they reached the door, she extricated her hand from his. "I've made it perfectly clear how I feel about your intervention, Caveman. I don't know why you think we need to discuss this further."

He took the gym bag from her tight grip, set it at their feet, then before she could stop him, took her into his arms. "I want you to hear my side of this."

"But—"

Placing his index finger to her lips, he shook his head. "For once in your life, will you stop arguing with me and listen?"

The feel of his arms around her, the sincere look in his hazel eyes, had her slowly nodding. "I'll give you five minutes, Yardley."

"Fair enough." He looked heavenward for a moment before once again meeting her gaze.

"Well?" she prompted when he hesitated.

"You want to shoot me a break here, Campbell? This isn't easy for me to admit." Taking a deep breath, he continued. "My stepping in to stop Valente from manhandling you had nothing to do with your competency as a federal agent, or with the case we're working on."

"Then what was the purpose?"

His mouth compressed into a flat line and she could tell he wasn't happy. "I don't want another man touching you."

Her breath caught. It had been the very last thing she'd expected him to say. "Would you...like to clarify what you mean by that?"

"I don't know that I understand it myself," he admitted. "I've never had this problem before." He released her to step away as he rubbed the back of his neck with an agitated hand. "And I'm not real sure that I like it. But the thought of another man putting his hands on you turns me wrong-side out."

"But you don't even like me."

"I never said that." He laughed, but the sound held little humor. "The problem is, I'm beginning to like you too much." Cole knew he was making a fool of himself, but he couldn't seem to stop, or to get his thoughts organized enough to make sense of what he was trying to tell her. "All I know is that when I saw Valente take hold of your arm, I wanted to tear him apart with my bare hands."

"I...don't know what to say." Elise looked as bewildered as he felt.

"That makes two of us, sweetheart." He met her green gaze and a warm feeling spread throughout his chest. "I'm sorry you thought I was undermining your authority, but that wasn't the case." He clamped his mouth shut and shrugged to keep from making an even bigger fool of himself. "I just wanted you to know that what I did wasn't out of any disrespect for your skills as an FBI agent.''

"Thank you," she said, sounding uncertain. "I appreciate your candidness." She stared at him for several long seconds before reaching down to pick up her pink and black gym bag. "I really need to…get back to work now."

He nodded, not sure whether to grab her and kiss her, or turn around and run as far and fast as his legs would carry him. Instead, he stood rooted to the spot. "Just be careful from now on, Campbell."

Nodding, she turned and started down the steps.

Cole watched her walk to the parking lot to make sure she got in the car and drove away without being accosted by Valente again. Then, shaking his head, he slowly walked back into the clubhouse.

"Damn, Yardley! You look like you just lost your best friend."

"Can it, Mercado. I'm not in the mood."

The man rocked back on his heels, looking thoughtful. "Did you and the pretty lady have a lovers' spat?" he asked.

"Agent Campbell and I are co-workers," Cole said tightly. He wasn't about to tell anyone otherwise.

"Then you won't mind my asking her to watch the fireworks with me this evening?" Mercado paused, then grinning, added, "After dark."

"Leave Elise alone," Cole growled before he could stop himself.

"Oh, so it's Elise, is it?" Mercado laughed. "You're mighty territorial about Special Agent Campbell. Are you sure she's not your lady?"

"Mind your own business, Mercado," Cole

growled as he marched toward the entrance to the Men's Grill.

"You didn't answer my question, Yardley," Mercado called after him.

Turning to face the man, Cole shook his head. "If you so much as give her the time of day, I'll have you jailed faster than you can slap your own ass with both hands."

Mercado threw back his head and laughed like a damn hyena, infuriating Cole further.

Without another word, he spun around and walked straight into the bar. What he needed was some peace and quiet, a six-pack of beer and some time to think. It was that, or he'd have to end up going to see the ATF's shrink as soon as he returned to Vegas to find out what the hell had gotten into him.

Elise sat in the middle of a patchwork quilt beneath the clear south Texas sky watching the twilight of evening slip into the dark of night. Everyone from Mission Creek was gathering on the country club's lawn for the fireworks display that the Lone Star put on every night during the summer festival.

After her run-in with John Valente and Cole's disturbing admission, she'd gone back to the inn and spent the rest of the afternoon, and most of the evening, thinking about what had happened earlier in the day. Cole was probably right about her not knowing how to deal with a man like John Valente. Most of her time was spent in an office behind a mountain of paperwork. She was only sent out in the field occasionally. Even though she'd had the training every other FBI operative had gone through, she simply didn't have the field experience to hone her skills and instincts.

But that wasn't what had prevented her from continuing to pore over the accounts of the former Mercado family heads and the records of the trucking and produce companies. It was Cole's admission that had kept her from being able to concentrate on finding the paper trail she was sure existed, linking the Mercados and their holdings to the gun smuggling.

On one hand, it was nice to know he was having as many unprofessional thoughts about her as she was having about him. But on the other hand, it went against every belief she had about co-workers never becoming romantically involved with each other.

Although, technically, she wasn't really working with Cole. He was an ATF agent, not FBI. He worked out of Las Vegas and she was assigned to a field office in Virginia. They weren't collaborating on the Mercado case. He'd said he worked alone—that he wasn't in the habit of sharing information. And so far, he'd been true to his word. He hadn't shared so much as a hint of a lead with her.

But that was just splitting hairs. They had both been assigned to the same case, even if their investigations were separate. And the fact that they had worked on cases in the past, and might do so again in the future, was a big factor to consider.

Unfortunately, the biggest, most important, reason that she couldn't let herself become romantically involved with Cole had nothing whatsoever to do with her golden rule and everything to do with guarding her heart. She had a feeling that if she didn't watch her step, she could fall head over heels for the man.

"Mind if I join you?"

At the sound of Cole's voice, she glanced up. Why all of a sudden did her heart pound as if she'd run a marathon? And why did just the sound of his sexy baritone send a wave of longing straight through her?

Staring up at him, Elise bit her lower lip to stifle her startled gasp. With crystal clarity, she knew exactly why her heart thudded in her chest like a jungle drum, and why every nerve in her body had come to full alert. She'd already fallen for Caveman Cole.

"Elise, are you all right?" he asked, squatting down beside her.

She might have been if he hadn't done the one thing that caused her to melt on the inside and stopped her from fighting the inevitable. He gently cupped her cheek with his hand.

Unable to speak, she finally managed to nod, hoping with all her heart that the storm of emotion and confusion clamoring inside her wasn't detectable in her expression.

"Are you sure?" he asked, looking concerned.

"Y-yes, I'm fine."

"Do you mind if I watch the fireworks with you?" he asked again, his voice surrounding her like a velvet caress.

She should rise to her feet, fold up the borrowed quilt and run. Instead, she nodded. "Cole, we need to discuss what you—"

"Not now," he said, sitting down behind her. He startled her when he planted his feet, one on each side of her, then pulled her back between his bent knees to nestle her against his chest.

Her skin tingled and her insides heated at the feel

of his strong arms wrapping her to hold her close. She looked at the other people sitting on the lawn. She didn't see John Valente, but it was dark now and that didn't mean he wasn't sitting close to her and Cole. "Are we putting on a show for Valente?"

"Nope," he whispered close to her ear. His warm breath sent goose bumps shimmering over her skin. "As far as I'm concerned, we're off duty tonight. It's not Agent Yardley and Special Agent Campbell. We're just Cole and Elise—two people enjoying each other's company."

"This is insane. We shouldn't be—"

"Hush," he said, kissing her temple. "We'll talk later. The fireworks are about to start."

A loud boom followed by a brilliant burst of twinkling sparks suddenly lit up the night sky above, signaling that the pyrotechnics show had indeed begun. A hush fell over the crowd as a continuous stream of colorful starbursts flashed overhead. Only the occasional voice of an excited child interrupted the otherwise intimate atmosphere surrounding them.

Even though the display was quite impressive, Elise barely noticed. She was too preoccupied with thoughts about what Cole was doing and the way he was making her feel. His warm strength surrounded her like a protective cloak and she suddenly didn't want to think about the Mercado crime family, the gun-smuggling ring, or the fact that she was walking all over her golden rule of not becoming involved with someone she worked with.

As a flash of blue and yellow fire streaked upward, then burst into a brilliant array of light, Cole pulled her more fully to him and slipped his hands beneath the tail of her white peasant blouse. Her breath caught. But when he caressed her abdomen, then cupped her breasts, she quit breathing completely.

"Wh-what are you doing?" she asked, trying to keep her voice from drawing attention to them.

"Shh, sweetheart. You'll miss the show."

"If anyone cared to look, they'd probably say *we're* putting on a show."

His deep chuckle vibrated straight through her. "Nobody's watching us." He nuzzled the hollow behind her ear. "And to tell you the truth, I don't give a damn if they are."

He unhooked the front clasp of her bra, and at the first touch of his warm palms holding her, her pulse leaped into overdrive. But when he chafed his thumbs over her tightened nipples, her heart skipped several beats and a coil of need began to form deep in the pit of her belly.

Closing her eyes, her head fell back against his shoulder and, heaven help her, she couldn't have stopped a tiny moan from escaping if her life depended on it.

"Does that feel good, sweetheart?" he whispered.

She nodded. "You shouldn't be doing this."

"Do you want me to stop?"

"Yes," she said, even as a betraying sigh of pure pleasure passed her lips.

He gently rolled the tight nubs between his thumbs and forefingers. "Are you sure?"

"No." She shook her head. "I mean, yes." Why was it suddenly so hard to think?

Sitting between his legs as she was, her bottom rested against his groin and she knew immediately when his body began to change, to harden with the same tension building inside her. She felt light-headed at the intensity of her own body's answering need.

Lost in the sensations Cole was creating, it surprised her when he suddenly pulled his hands from beneath her blouse and turned her in his arms. Arranging her legs over one of his, he cradled her to him, then gazed down at her a moment before he lowered his head and placed his mouth on hers.

At first he nibbled and caressed, but when his tongue traced the fullness of her lower lip, she raised up to meet his kiss. Wrapping her arms around his neck, she parted for him and completely surrendered herself to his exploration. Had she been able to think, her eager response would have shocked her. But at the moment, rational thought was beyond her capabilities. All she wanted to do was feel Cole tasting her, tantalizing her senses with his gentle coaxing.

Elise's passionate response to his kiss sent blood surging through Cole's veins and his arousal was so intense that he felt dizzy. He wanted her with a hunger that shocked him, and he knew for certain he was treading in an area he'd never been before. He wanted to join their bodies, but more than that, he felt a deep need to join their souls—to once and for all make her his.

That should have scared the hell out of him. But the feel of her soft body in his arms, the taste of her sweet lips beneath his, had him feeling as if he could move mountains with his bare hands.

Raising his head to gaze down at her, he smiled. ''Damn, sweetheart, I want you so bad I can't think straight.''

As he stared down at her a starburst lit the night sky and illuminated her pretty face. The desire coloring her porcelain cheeks, the urgent need in her green eyes, had his heart beating against his ribs like an out-of-control jackhammer.

"Let's go back to the inn," he said suddenly.

She stared at him for what seemed like an eternity before she slowly nodded her head and untangled her legs from his.

Cole rose to his feet and held his hand out to help her up from the quilt they'd been sitting on. When she started to fold the coverlet, he took it from her, wadded it up and tucked it under one arm. Taking her hand in his, he led her through the maze of people sitting in lawn chairs and on blankets.

Once they reached her car, he drew her close for a quick kiss. "I'll follow you to the inn."

Waiting until she closed the door and locked it, he jogged over to where he'd parked the SUV and got in. He'd done a lot of thinking after she'd left him this afternoon and decided he had one of two choices. He could try ignoring the magnetic pull between them, and quickly lose his mind. Or he could give in to the chemistry, enjoy the time they had together here in Mission Creek, and worry about his sanity once he returned to Vegas.

And who knew what might happen? There was always the possibility that after they returned to their respective offices, they might make arrangements to spend an occasional weekend together when they both had time off.

When he steered the SUV into the inn parking lot, he parked beside Elise's rental car, got out and walked over to help her from the sedan. As soon as he opened the driver's door, he knew that she was having second thoughts.

"Cole, I don't think our sleeping together would be wise," she said without preamble.

He took a deep breath, then another as he reconciled himself to a cold shower and an empty bed. Nodding, he placed his hand at her back to guide her through the front doors of the inn. "You're probably right."

They both remained silent as they rode the elevator to the second floor.

When they walked down the hall and stopped in front of Elise's door, she smiled sadly. "We'd only be complicating things that until now have been relatively simple."

He wasn't sure who she was trying to convince, him or herself. Stuffing his hands into his jeans pockets to keep from reaching for her, he nodded. "I couldn't agree more."

She gazed up at him for a moment before turning to open her door. "I...um, good night."

"Night," he said, walking the few feet that separated his door from hers.

He'd wanted nothing more than to take her into his arms and kiss her senseless, to make her want him again the way he still wanted her. But he knew that would be a mistake. She'd only end up regretting in the morning what they shared tonight.

Opening his door, he walked into the room and stood for several long seconds, staring at the door between their rooms. Even though Elise's body was telling her it was ready to take that step with him, her mind hadn't yet come to grips with what he recognized as the inevitable.

It wasn't a question of if they made love. It was just a matter of when.

Elise closed her eyes and tried to concentrate on her golden rule. *Thou shalt not get cozy with a coworker.*

Maybe if she repeated it enough, she'd be able to remember why she'd adopted that rule, and why it was so important. But at the moment, she couldn't think of a single reason why she'd embraced that philosophy.

Cole wanted her and she wanted him with a fierceness that stole her breath. All she'd have to do is open the door between their two rooms and—

Elise opened her eyes and frantically glanced around the room. Why was she even thinking along those lines?

Moaning, she threw back the sheet, sat up on the edge of the bed and took several deep breaths to calm herself. This was Caveman Cole causing her to lose sleep. They couldn't be in the same room for more than five minutes before they were engaged in a battle of wits.

But as she sat there trying to decipher her puzzling emotions, she remembered the warmth of his kiss, the feel of his hands caressing her body. Her breath caught and she felt as if she might be drowning as realization dawned. Had the sizzling attraction between them been there all along, hidden behind a veil of verbal sparring?

Lost in her disturbing thoughts, she jumped when the door between her room and Cole's opened.

"You can't sleep, either?" Cole asked, walking over to stand in front of her.

The sight of him standing there in nothing but his briefs made her feel warm all over and had her feminine places tingling as they'd never tingled before. "I...I—" She had to pause to get her scrambled thoughts off his magnificent body and onto what he'd asked her. "No. I can't seem to get comfortable."

He shook his head. "Me, neither. I can't seem to forget how sweet your kisses are, or how you feel when I hold you." Rubbing the back of his neck with his hand, he gazed down at her. "It's crazy, but I want you more now than I've ever wanted any woman in my life."

His admission made her heart skip several beats. "I couldn't agree more. It's completely insane."

"Then tell me to leave you alone and get the hell out of here."

Was that what she really wanted? To tell him to go back to his room? Alone?

Rising to her feet, she took a deep breath. "I can't do that, Cole."

She heard his sharp intake of breath, saw his hazel eyes darken. "Why, Elise? Why can't you tell me to leave?"

Her pulse pounded in her ears and she felt as if she was about to jump off a cliff without knowing what awaited her below. But she couldn't think about that now. All she knew was that she'd never wanted anything more in her life than to have Cole holding her, loving her.

"I can't tell you to go because I don't have the strength," she said softly. "And I can't fight it any longer. Please make love to me, Cole."

Seven

"Are you sure?" Cole asked, not at all certain he wanted her to answer his question. If she said she wasn't, he didn't think Mission Creek had enough water in their reservoir for the cold shower he'd need to take.

The smile she gave him nearly knocked him to his knees. "That's the only thing I'm sure of."

He reached out and pulled her to him. Covering her mouth with his, he kissed her until they both gasped for air. "Let's go into my room, sweetheart," he said, swinging her up into his arms.

She put her arms around his shoulders to steady herself, then gave him a puzzled look. "Why on earth are you carrying me?"

"Because that's what a caveman does when he drags a woman off to his cave," he said, grinning as he walked through the door into his room.

"I thought they dragged a woman by her hair," she said, smiling. He loved the tiny dimples that appeared at the sides of her mouth when she smiled.

"Your hair is too short." Setting her on her feet beside his bed, he reached out to tangle his fingers in the soft auburn curls. "And it's too soft and pretty to do that." He smiled. "Besides, the last thing I'd ever do is hurt you in any way, Elise."

He kissed her forehead, her eyes and the tip of her nose before lowering his mouth to hers. Her lips were soft, moist and sweeter than anything he'd ever tasted.

"I want to kiss you all over, sweetheart," he said hoarsely. As he nipped his way down her throat to her delicate collarbone, he worked the buttons of her nightshirt through the buttonholes.

When he parted the satin lapels, his breath lodged in his lungs. "You're perfect."

Taking the weight of her breasts in his palms, he chafed the tight tips with his thumbs as he watched her eyes close and her head fall back. "Does that feel good, sweetheart?"

She raised her head and opened her eyes to look at him. The desire he detected in her clear gaze caused his mouth to go dry. "I love the feel of you caressing me." Smiling, she brought her hands up to glide over his shoulders and pectoral muscles. "I've wanted to do this since we were at the pool this morning."

Her delicate touch caused the muscles in his lower abdomen and groin to tighten. "You have no idea how good that feels."

"I think I do," she said, glancing down at the bulge straining against his cotton briefs.

He chuckled. "You're making it kind of hard to

hide, sweetheart." He slipped the nightshirt from her creamy shoulders, then stepped back to look at her. When he lifted his gaze to hers, he thought she looked a bit uncertain. Her vulnerability touched him in ways he'd never have believed possible. "You're beautiful, Elise."

"So are you," she said, placing her soft hand on his cheek.

Taking her into his arms, he pulled her to him and the feel of her breasts pressed to his chest sent a tremor of need coursing through him. Her hands skimming over his back and down his flanks was heaven and hell rolled into one. But when she traced the waistband of his briefs with her slender fingers, Cole's heart thudded so hard that he wouldn't have been surprised if it cracked a couple of ribs.

"I think we'd better lie down before my knees give out," he said, lowering her to the mattress. He leaned down to give her a quick kiss. "I'll be right back."

When he returned from the bathroom with their protection, he slipped the foil packet beneath his pillow, then stretched out beside her. Propping himself up on one elbow, he leaned over her to kiss her with every emotion he had but couldn't put a name to.

Elise wrapped her arms around Cole's neck and gave herself up to his masterful kiss. Tonight she'd forget that she was an FBI agent and Cole was an ATF operative. Tonight they were simply a woman and man coming together to explore the magnetic pull between them that could no longer be denied.

When she parted her lips, he slipped his tongue inside to mimic a more intimate coupling, and ribbons of desire quickly spiraled throughout her being to twine into a tight coil of need deep in her belly. He brought his hand up to cup her breast and his gentle caress sent a shiver of longing straight through her. But when he moved his hand along her side to the indentation of her waist and beyond, Elise moaned and moved restlessly beneath his tender touch.

He slowly slid his hand down to her knee, then back up along the inside of her thigh. A ripple of excitement coursed through her when his fingers slipped inside the leg of her panties to tease her with a featherlight touch.

Wanting to explore his body as he was hers, she brought her hands down to trace the cords of his strong neck, to measure his wide shoulders. His hard, male body felt absolutely wonderful beneath her fingers and she found it just as arousing to touch him as it was to have him touch her.

He shuddered against her as she glided her palms over his back to the elastic band of his briefs. When she dipped her fingers inside to test the tight muscles of his buttocks, his groan of pleasure vibrated against her lips.

"I think you're killing me," he said, sounding short of breath. His own fingers slid beneath the lace band of her panties. "Lift your hips, sweetheart."

When she did as he commanded, he whisked the scrap of silk away in one smooth motion, then rose up to allow her to do the same with his briefs. The feel of his hard, hair-roughened body against hers sent an electric current skipping over every nerve in her body when he once again lowered himself to cover her.

His lips heated her skin as he rained tiny kisses

from her collarbone down the slope of her breast at the same time he slid his hand between them to touch the tight nest of curls at the juncture of her thighs. As he took the taut tip into his mouth to tenderly suck on it, he parted her to gently touch her femininity, and Elise thought she would go up in flames from the exquisite pleasure of it.

Restless with a need to give to him as he gave to her, she moved her hand between them to circle his hard maleness. A low groan rumbled up from deep in his chest when she explored his strength and the velvet softness below.

"Sweetheart, I'll give you all night to not stop that," he said, raising his head to grin down at her. But as she continued to stroke him, his eyes closed and his easy expression faded. Reaching down, he took her hand in his. "Maybe that's not such a good idea after all."

"But I thought you said I could do this all night," she said, wondering if that throaty female voice was really hers.

When he moved his own hand lower and slipped one finger inside her, all thought instantly ceased and she couldn't have stopped her moan of pleasure if her life depended on it.

"Cole, I—"

Nuzzling the sensitive hollow behind her ear, he whispered, "Tell me what you want, sweetheart."

"Y-you."

He kissed her so tenderly that it brought tears to her eyes, then reached for the foil packet that she'd seen him place under his pillow earlier. Once he'd arranged their protection, he took her into his arms, nudged her legs apart with his knee, and holding her gaze with his, he moved to settle himself over her.

Her body welcomed him as he slowly, carefully, pushed forward and sank himself deep within her. Staring down at her, his hazel eyes darkened to chocolate brown. "You feel so damn good, sweetheart. So…tight." She felt a shudder run through his much larger frame. "I don't think I can wait much longer," he said, his voice filled with the strain of holding himself in check. "Are you…all right?"

"I'm…wonderful," she said, wrapping her arms around him.

When she tilted her hips, she felt him sink farther into her. He groaned and set a slow, easy pace that quickly had her biting her lower lip to keep from crying out. The consideration Cole was showing her, the care with which he moved inside of her caused her heart to swell with emotion. She'd never felt more cherished in her entire life.

As the feelings built, he quickened his thrusts and Elise felt herself rapidly climbing the peak of fulfillment. Her body strained to be closer to him, to absorb him into her very soul. Never had lovemaking been so compelling, so all-consuming that she forgot where she ended and he began.

Reaching the pinnacle, the coil inside her stomach tightened to an almost unbearable ache a moment before the spiral within her snapped and wave after exquisite wave of pleasure overtook her. Almost immediately, Cole tensed, then as he gave in to the force of his own climax, his body quaked as he filled her with his essence. When his storm was finally spent, he collapsed on top of her, burying his face in the side of her neck.

She held him to her and reveled in the feel of his weight pressing her into the mattress, the heat that radiated from him. Even though she'd tried to deny it, had fought against it, she could no longer deny that she'd fallen in love with Cole.

He nuzzled the side of her neck. "I'm too heavy for you."

"No…you feel…good," she said, fighting the tears that threatened to slip down her cheeks.

Her wavering voice must have alerted him. "What's wrong?" he asked, levering himself up on his elbows. "Did I hurt you?"

The concern on his handsome face, the apprehension she detected in his voice, caused a tear to slip from the corner of her eyes. "No."

"Then what's wrong, sweetheart?" He gently brushed a curl from her forehead as he searched her face. "Talk to me, Elise."

Swallowing around the lump in her throat, she gave him a watery smile. "That was beautiful."

His own smile warmed her heart as he shook his head. "I'll agree that it was pretty good, but I wanted you too much to take the time I should have." He kissed the tip of her nose. "I promise that next time will be even better."

"Better?"

"Much better," he said, grinning as he rolled to her side. Almost immediately his easy expression disappeared and he sucked in a sharp breath as he jerked upright in bed. "Oh, hell!"

Alarmed, Elise sat up and grabbed the sheet and wrapped it around herself. "Are you okay?"

"We…may have a problem," he said hesitantly.

The apologetic look in his eyes sent a shiver of fear snaking down her spine. "What's wrong?"

"The condom broke." She watched him close his eyes and take a deep breath. When he opened them, he looked straight into hers. "Tell me you're on the Pill."

"N-no. There was no reason. I haven't been intimate with anyone since…" Her voice trailed off.

"Since when?" he prompted.

She felt her cheeks heat. Answering questions about her love life, or more accurately, the lack of one, wasn't something she envisioned discussing after the most incredible experience of her life.

"I'm afraid I've not got a lot of…experience. I…haven't been intimate with anyone since college."

As the gravity of the situation hit her, she bit her lower lip to keep it from trembling. What if she became pregnant?

He must have noticed her concern, because he reached out and took her into his arms. "Sweetheart, I'm sorry. I didn't mean to sound like I was interrogating you." He kissed the top of her head as he held her to him. "I only asked because if you do become pregnant, there's no question that I'll be the father."

Hoping she was right, she tried for a light tone. "I'm pretty sure the odds are against that happening."

"You're probably right." He released her to cup her face with both of his large hands. "But I want you to know that if you do get pregnant, we'll face it together. I'll be there for you every step of the way.''

The sincerity she detected in his gaze left her with no doubt he meant what he said. Now. But what about the day-to-day responsibility of caring for a child? It was one thing to face up to financial obligations, but would he be available for decisions concerning illness, schooling, discipline? Or would she be on her own to juggle the many demands of motherhood and her career with the Bureau?

She closed her eyes against the questions making her head spin. There was no sense in speculating about something that in all likelihood wasn't even a concern.

''Would you hand me my nightshirt, please?'' she asked, pointing to the garment lying by the side of the bed.

He looked puzzled. ''Why?''

''I think it would be best if I went back to my room.''

''I don't.'' It wasn't the answer she'd expected.

''Why not?''

''You don't need to be alone right now. You'll only end up worrying the rest of the night about what might happen.'' Pulling her onto his lap, he cradled her to his wide chest, then touched her cheek with his index finger. ''It's out of our control now, sweetheart. There's no sense dwelling on it.'' He kissed her with such tenderness it felt as if her insides had turned to Jell-O. ''Spend the night here, with me.''

His strong arms holding her so securely, the feel of his gentle touch, and his reassuring words had her feeling as if she never wanted to move. And he was

right. She would lie awake thinking of all the what-
ifs, when what she really wanted was to be wrapped
in his warm embrace.

"If I sleep in your bed, I'll still need my nightshirt."

He shook his head and the wicked grin he gave her
sent a shaft of longing straight to the pit of her belly.
"I really prefer what you're wearing now."

She laughed. "A sheet?"

"No. A smile."

Holding Elise close, Cole lay awake long after she
fell asleep. What if he had made her pregnant? Was
he ready to be a father? Would he be good at par-
enting? How would he even know if he was or
wasn't?

All he had to go by was his own upbringing, and
that was anything but normal. Raised by a marine
sergeant, moving from place to place whenever
Gunny received new orders, wasn't much to go by.

But his father had done the best he could, and in-
stilled Cole with values that had served him well over
the past thirty years. He'd always been on the right
side of the law, served his country with dignity and
honor, and been an honest, upright citizen. Weren't
those qualities that any man would be proud to pass
along to his child?

His child.

Those two words should have him nervous enough
to jump out of his own skin. But all things considered,
he was pretty damn calm about the possibility of Elise
being pregnant.

Glancing down at her head pillowed on his shoulder, he wondered how she would feel about having his baby? Would she embrace motherhood?

When she stirred in her sleep and murmured his name, his chest filled with a warmth that he couldn't explain and didn't dare try to analyze. Time would give him the answers to his questions and end his speculation. All he had to do was wait.

Yawning, he smiled as he drifted on the edge of sleep. In the meantime, he'd wrap up his investigation and arrest whoever was responsible for smuggling guns into Mezcaya.

And every night for as long as they were together in Mission Creek, he'd concentrate on making love to the most desirable woman he'd ever met.

Elise sat up straight and studied the column of figures on the Mercado Trucking Company's computer printout. They were hauling freight all the way to Mezcaya for the Superior Produce Company. That in itself wasn't unusual. Mercado Trucking was the largest freight hauler outside of Corpus Christi, and Superior was the only produce company in the tricounty area.

On the surface, everything looked to be in order. But what had every one of her auditing instincts on full alert was the amount of money Superior Produce had been writing off as spoilage. Why would a company continue to export their product when three-quarters of it went bad before it even arrived?

None of it made sense, unless—

Elise smiled. "I think I've found my lead."

"What was that?" Cole called through the open door between their two rooms.

Confident that she'd found the break she'd been looking for, she wrote down the figures displayed on her calculator screen, then switched it off. She'd been working all day and most of the evening. She needed a break.

Walking into Cole's room, she shook her head. "I was talking to myself."

Sitting on the bed with his back propped up against the headboard, he patted the mattress beside his outstretched legs. "I thought you might have discovered the link between the guns and the Mercados."

"Like I'd tell you," she said, laughing.

By unspoken agreement, they'd kept their personal relationship separate from their work. They still weren't sharing information, and she doubted that they would. The focus of her investigation was on the paper trail, while Cole was involved with collecting physical evidence.

When she sat down beside him, he reached out to take her hand in his. "What do you say we order something from room service and spend the rest of the evening right here?"

"You don't want to go out to the country club for tonight's summer festival?" she asked, her insides heating from the look in his sexy gaze.

He shook his head as he pulled her onto his lap. "I spent the entire day at the Lone Star, dogging Mercado from the golf course, to the billiards room, then to a poker game in the Men's Grill. I've had enough of that place for a while."

"Did you discover anything?" she asked, knowing he wouldn't tell her if he did.

"Yep," he said, surprising her.

"What did you find out?"

"I found out how much I missed you." He kissed her forehead. "I kept thinking about last night and the promise I made to you."

"Promise?" Was he going to tell her that he'd changed his mind? That if she did become pregnant she'd be on her own?

"Don't you remember?" he asked, smiling. "I told you that the next time we made love would be even better." He slipped his hand beneath the bottom of her T-shirt. "I didn't get to show you."

His warm palm caressing her abdomen sent a flash of tingling heat to every nerve in her body. "You don't want to watch the fireworks? Tonight's the last—"

He shook his head. "I'd much rather stay here and create fireworks with you."

When Cole's mouth came down on hers, Elise forgot all about the country club's festivities as his firm lips nibbled and coaxed, caressed and teased her with a mastery that stole her breath. But when his tongue parted her lips to deepen the kiss, it felt as if a few pyrotechnics had indeed been set off in her soul.

Flickers of light danced behind her closed eyes and heat flowed through her veins like warm honey as he stroked the inner recesses of her mouth, played a game of advance and retreat with his tongue. The feel of his palm taking the weight of her bare breast, his thumb brushing her hardened nipple, ignited a spark of desire inside her that quickly turned into a flame of deep need.

Cole broke the kiss to whisk Elise's shirt off, then lowered his head to take the beaded tip of her breast into his mouth. Her sweet taste, the feel of the nub tightening as he drew on it deeply, sent his blood pressure skyrocketing.

He lowered her to the mattress, savoring the way she held his head to her, how she sighed softly when he moved to pay homage to the other soft mound. Bringing her pleasure was as arousing as any aphrodisiac and it came as no surprise that he was harder than he'd ever been in his life.

When she tugged at his T-shirt, he raised his head. "I didn't hurt you, did I?"

"No, but don't you think you're a bit overdressed?" she asked, sounding delightfully breathless.

He chuckled. "You might be right." Rising from the bed, he quickly dispensed with his shirt, jeans and briefs, then lay back down beside her. "Now who's the one overdressed?"

"I suppose that would be me." The smile she gave him caused a fire to ignite in his belly. "So what are you going to do about it?"

"Give me a minute and I'll show you," he said, working the button free at the top of her cutoff jeans.

Slowly sliding the zipper down, he held her gaze with his as he pulled her shorts and panties down her slender hips and long legs, then tossed the garments aside. Leaning over, he pressed his mouth to her flat stomach. "Your skin is like fine satin, sweetheart. So smooth, so soft."

He felt a tremor course through her when he kissed his way down one leg. But when he pressed his lips to the inner part of her thigh, she gasped. "You... shouldn't."

"Why not?" he asked, continuing his exploration.

"No one's ever—"

"Do you trust me, Elise?"

To his satisfaction she didn't hesitate. "Yes."

"Then let me love you all over, sweetheart." Finding her, he took pleasure in her soft moans as he gave her what no man had given to her before.

"P-please, Cole." She moved restlessly against him. "I can't stand…much more."

When he raised his head, he didn't think he'd ever seen a more beautiful sight than the blush of passion on her porcelain cheeks, the hunger in her expressive green eyes. "Tell me what you need, Elise."

"Y-you. Now!"

Her desire fueled his own and he was suddenly consumed with the need to once again make her his. Opening the drawer of the nightstand, he removed a foil packet he'd placed there earlier and took care of their protection.

Turning back, his breath lodged in his lungs at the sight of her supple body waiting to take him in and make him feel as if he'd found the other half of himself. The sudden hunger to possess her once again was overwhelming.

Cole closed his eyes for a moment in a desperate attempt to regain his rapidly slipping control. He was going to make this the most memorable night of her life, if it killed him. And he wasn't sure that it wouldn't.

His pulse pounded in his ears as he moved over her, and gathering her in his arms, joined their bodies in one smooth stroke. He held himself completely still as he tried to resist the urge to complete the act of loving her. He wanted to make this last, to love her slowly and thoroughly.

But when she wrapped her long legs around his hips to draw him in and hold him to her, Cole's restraint snapped and his mind clouded with a red haze of need. Rocking against her, he reveled in the way she met him stroke for stroke, their bodies perfectly in tune. But when he felt her tighten around him, he knew she was close to the culmination they both sought. Quickening his pace, a deep satisfaction flowed through him at her cry of pleasure as she found the ecstasy of her release.

Her feminine muscles clinging to him, urging him to find his own climax, drove Cole over the edge, and he felt as if they became one mind, one body, one soul as he emptied his life force deep inside of her.

Eight

The next afternoon, Cole drove out to the western edge of Mission Creek where several abandoned warehouses were located. He'd been meaning to check them out for the past couple of days, but he'd been too busy interviewing all of the Lone Star Country Club's employees with access to the storage building where the guns had been found.

But he had a hunch those weapons had been planted at the country club in an effort to divert attention from the hub of the actual smuggling operation. Now all he had to do was find evidence to support his theory.

He parked the SUV in front of a group of four warehouses that looked as if they hadn't been used in years. Getting out of the truck, he walked from one to another. Nothing looked out of the ordinary. Scrub brush grew in front of the doors, and most of the windows had been broken out of the first two buildings. But when he rounded the corner of the second dilapidated structure, he stopped short. The glint of sunlight bouncing off the big double doors caught his attention and his investigative instincts came to full alert. The corrugated metal was covered in rust, but something shiny appeared to be wrapped around the door handles.

As he walked the distance between the two buildings, several things seemed to jump out at him. The first was the tire tracks scoring the hard-packed dirt leading up to the doors, indicating that the vehicle making them had been heavy. He knelt down, and examining the double tread marks, Cole determined they had most likely been made by a semi with a loaded trailer.

Straightening, he continued on to check out the doors of the warehouse. A thick chain was threaded through the pulls on the door and had been secured with a heavy padlock. Both were new. When the toe of his boot touched some of the scrub brush in front of the doors, he noticed that it and several others had been placed to look as if they were growing there.

He walked around the outside of the building, finding several fresh cigarette butts along the perimeter. He smiled as he pulled a small plastic bag from his pocket, and careful not to touch it, scooped one of the butts into it. He'd send it to the lab for testing to see if they already had a DNA profile on whoever had smoked the cigarette.

He had a feeling he just got the first break in the

case. He'd stake his reputation on this being the actual hub of the gun-smuggling operation.

After he'd made a trip back to the SUV for a digital camera, he took several shots of the tire tracks, the padlocked door and the outside of the building. Now all he had to do was find out who owned the warehouses and get a warrant to search the property.

But as he drove back into town, his discovery left a bittersweet taste in his mouth. On one hand, he felt sure he was on the verge of cracking the case. But on the other, it would mean his time with Elise was close to ending.

His gut clenched at the thought of not having her in his arms each night, or waking up to see her pretty face first thing each morning. He took a deep breath. How had she gotten under his skin so fast? Had it really started a week ago when he saw John Valente take hold of her arm in front of the country club? Or had it started long before that?

When they'd worked on the same case two years ago, he'd thought Elise was a looker with a killer smile and the best legs he'd ever seen. But they hadn't been able to stay in the same room for more than ten minutes without getting into a verbal battle of one-upmanship.

He smiled. But as much as he'd groused about her sharp tongue, he'd enjoyed those encounters. Elise was quick-witted, intelligent and a damn fine federal agent. In fact, her auditing skills had been instrumental in cracking that case in El Paso.

His easy expression disappeared. As far as he was concerned, her job was a blessing and a curse all rolled into one. It had been the reason for their meeting, and what had brought them together again on the Lone Star case. But it was also what bothered him the most about her. The thought that she might, at some time, have to draw her gun or use her physical-defense skills to fend off some goon like Valente just about turned Cole's stomach. What would happen if he wasn't around to intervene?

Turning into the courthouse parking lot, he killed the engine and sat for several long minutes, contemplating what he needed to do. His only option to keep Elise safe was to crack this case, take the gun smugglers into custody, and hopefully put the Mercado crime family out of business in the process, while she was still holed up at the inn crunching numbers.

He started to get out of the SUV, then glanced at his watch. Damn! By the time he walked up to the courthouse entrance it would be closing for the day.

Settling himself back behind the steering wheel, he started the Explorer and backed out of the parking space. He'd have to check with the clerk's office tomorrow to see who held the deed to the warehouse property. Right now, he intended to go back to the inn, take Elise into his arms and make love to her until they both collapsed from exhaustion.

Elise glanced at the figures in front of her, then at the calculator screen. There was no doubt in her mind that Mercado Trucking and Superior Produce were somehow involved in the gun smuggling, either by transporting the contraband, or laundering the money from the sales. Or both. Superior had been using Mercado Trucking to ship fruits and vegetables into Mezcaya on a regular basis, but still hadn't shown a profit.

The trucking company bills of lading showed that they were hauling bananas, coffee and sugar. Now, why would Superior be importing things into a country that was a major exporter of those very same items?

But how could she prove the link between the Mercado owned companies and the automatic weapons being smuggled into Mezcaya? She needed to know exactly what was being hauled in those trucks, and the only way she knew to do that was to be there when a shipment arrived to see what was unloaded.

She tapped the ink pen she held on the polished surface of the desk as she checked the dates on the trucking company's books. If they were correct, another shipment should be arriving in Mezcaya this weekend.

Taking a deep breath, she reached for the phone. She'd have to clear the trip with her superiors, but that shouldn't be a problem. Her boss had told her to do whatever it took to uncover the evidence needed to crack the case.

An hour later, she hung up the phone with a satisfied smile. She'd made airline reservations and was set to go. Day after tomorrow she would be leaving for Mezcaya.

Once she entered the tiny Central American country, she would meet an undercover operative at the airport who would act as her guide and interpreter. He would take her to the jungle villages reported to have strong El Jefé connections, where she would pose as a buyer for an export company in search of handmade baskets, pottery and other native crafts.

She wasn't supposed to take any action while she

was in Mezcaya, just keep her eyes and ears open to see if she could find out what those trucks were really hauling. She'd have three days to learn all she could before returning to Mission Creek to hand over everything to the Special Operations Group. They would be the ones in charge of surveilling the suspects' activities, building the case against them, then, when the time was right, moving in to make the arrest.

There were only three things she had left to do. The first two were easy. She'd call the bank and have them release Ricky Mercado's assets, since it was obvious by his accounting records that he wasn't involved in the gun smuggling. Then she'd call him and tell him he was free to go on with his life.

The third, and most important, of her tasks wasn't going to be nearly as easy. How on earth was she going to break the news about her trip to Cole?

She suspected that once he learned she was leaving for Mezcaya day after tomorrow, he'd go caveman on her and try to prevent her from going. Or worse yet, he'd try to go with her. And as much as she loved being held by him, loved by him each night, the last thing she needed was him insisting that he accompany her to Central America.

Elise sighed and leaned back in the desk chair. Besides, she needed time away from him, time to come to grips with the idea that she might very well be carrying his baby.

Rising to her feet, she walked over to where her purse sat on the bureau and reached inside the leather bag for her personal calendar. Her period wasn't due to start until early next week, and it was too soon to purchase one of the early home-pregnancy tests.

But something deep inside told her that a test was just a formality. No matter how unlikely the odds were that she'd become pregnant the night the condom broke, she had a feeling that she had indeed conceived a child.

She placed her hand on her flat stomach. What if she was expecting? How would she tell Cole? What would he do? Would he want to get married?

She bit her lower lip to keep it from trembling. If they ever took that step, how would she know if he was asking her to be his wife because he loved her, or because he felt an obligation to the baby?

Whether she and Cole got married, or she ended up raising their son or daughter alone, she'd have to adjust her goals. There was no way she'd be able to travel and work cases like the one she was working on now.

"What's wrong, sweetheart?" Cole asked, coming to stand beside her. "You look awfully serious."

Some FBI agent she was, she thought disgustedly. He'd opened the door between their two rooms and walked right up to her without her even realizing it.

Turning to put her arms around his neck, she shook off her pensive mood. She'd have plenty of time on the plane ride down to Mezcaya to analyze everything and decide what she needed to do. Right now, she wanted to forget what the future held for them, and concentrate on the here and now.

"There's nothing wrong, Caveman," she said, going up on tiptoe to place a kiss on his firm male lips. "I was just thinking about what Mrs. Carter will say if we order room service again tonight, instead of going down for dinner."

"Probably not a damn thing," he said, grinning. "More than likely, she's in danger of breaking an arm from patting herself on the back for getting us together."

Elise wondered if they really were "together." Not sure she wanted to know the answer, she asked, "So what are we going to order this evening?"

"It doesn't matter," he said, nuzzling her neck. "Mrs. Carter will send two plates of whatever she wants us to have for dinner anyway."

"That's true. I keep ordering a salad, and she keeps sending me country-fried steak, or fried chicken, or fried pork chops. I don't think Mrs. Carter has read the latest articles on fried foods, cholesterol and weight management." Elise frowned. "I'll be lucky if I don't gain twenty pounds while I'm here in Mission Creek."

The look Cole gave her caused her toes to curl into the thick carpet. "You don't have to worry about your weight." He brushed his lips over hers. "You'd be desirable no matter what you weighed."

He said that now, but what if she was pregnant? Would he still find her attractive then?

But the thought of how she would look when she was heavy with his child deserted her as he kissed his way to the hollow behind her ear.

"I'm hungry," he murmured against her skin. Raising his head, he gazed down at her. "But not for food."

Her breath caught at the longing she saw in his hazel eyes, the feel of his arousal pressing into her lower belly. He brought his hands up beneath the bottom of her shirt to splay across her back, then pulled her more fully into his embrace.

Lowering his mouth to hers, he kissed her with a gentleness that made her weak in the knees and had her clinging to his strong biceps for support. His tongue traced her lips, then coaxed her to open for his entry. The taste of his need, the feel of him stroking the tender recesses sent shivers of desire spiraling through every cell in her body.

As he continued to kiss her, Cole moved his hands upward, taking her shirt with them. "Lift your arms, sweetheart."

Without giving a thought to protesting, she did as he commanded and he drew the garment over her head. Tossing it aside, he ran his palms over her shoulders, her back, then down her sides to her hips with such reverence that she felt light-headed. It was as if he worshiped her with his touch.

"I love it when you don't bother wearing a bra," he said, smiling as he skimmed his hands along the sides of her breasts.

"I've always thought of them as instruments of torture," she said shakily. "Especially the ones with underwire."

Reaching up, she traced the ATF initials on the middle of his T-shirt. The muscles beneath the fabric bunched and flexed as she drew her finger over each letter. "I love you in these black shirts."

"I told you I looked good in them," he said, mischievously. His breathing sounded labored.

Elise touched the sleeve where the knit stretched over his rock-hard biceps. "This is one time I have to agree with you, Caveman. You look extremely good in them.''

He reached down to pull the tail of the shirt from his jeans, then up and over his head. He tossed the garment on top of her shirt. ''As good as I look in it, there are times when I think I like being out of it a whole lot more.''

When he pulled her to his bare chest, she had to agree. The feel of her breasts crushed to his hard maleness quickly heated her blood and she suddenly felt warm all over. But when he leaned back and lowered his head to take one of the pebbled tips into his mouth, the warmth flowing though her veins turned to liquid fire.

Unable to resist, she placed her hands on his broad chest, testing the strength of his pectoral muscles, lightly running her fingers over his nipples. The tips puckered at her touch and she felt a shudder run through his big body at the same time he sucked in a sharp breath.

''Do you like that?'' she asked.

''Sw-sweetheart…'' Straightening to his full height, he stopped to clear his throat. ''You have no idea.''

With their lower bodies pressed so closely together, she could feel his hard arousal straining against his fly. ''Oh, I think I might have a vague notion, Caveman.''

She ran her index finger down his smooth chest and flat belly to the indentation of his navel, then continued down the thin line of hair that disappeared beneath the waistband of his jeans. Jeans that rode low on his narrow hips and exposed a nice amount of lean flanks.

Tugging at his belt, she worked the leather strap through the buckle, then toyed with the button at the top of his jeans. When she glanced up at him, the look in his heavy-lidded eyes challenged her to continue.

His stomach contracted when her fingers brushed his skin as she worked the button through the hole, then ran her nail down the metal teeth of his zipper, over the insistent bulge, then back up to the tab. Encouraged by his groan of pleasure, Elise eased it down and slowly opened the metal closure holding him captive.

"You're about to give me a heart attack," he said, his voice sounding like a rusty hinge.

Encouraged by the passion he couldn't hide, she ran her finger along the elastic band of his briefs. "Maybe I should stop."

"I don't think that would be a good idea."

"You don't?"

He shook his head. "I'll spontaneously combust, and you wouldn't want that on your conscience. Would you?"

"No, I don't suppose I would." She pretended to think for a minute. "But I don't want to cause you to have problems with your heart, either."

He laughed. "This kind of ailment has a pretty simple remedy."

"Oh, really?" She touched the hard bulge threatening to burst the white cotton fabric. "Do you think I might have the cure?"

"Sweetheart, you're the only cure for what ails me," he said, nodding. "So don't stop now."

Her heart stuttered. From the look he was giving her, she believed he was quite serious.

Taking a deep breath, she carefully pushed his jeans and briefs down over his hips, freeing him from the restraining garments. He placed his hands on her shoulders to steady himself as she shoved his clothes to his feet. Luckily he'd removed his boots before entering her room. That was probably the reason she hadn't heard him enter, she decided as she threw his clothes on top of their shirts.

She turned back and her breath caught at the sight of him. Cole was magnificent in his masculinity. His shoulders and chest were broad with well-defined muscles, his stomach ridged.

But when her gaze drifted lower, her pulse hammered in her ears. His size, the sheer strength of his need, was almost overwhelming. Feminine power flowed through her as she realized his desire, the depth of his longing, was for her.

"You're truly beautiful," she said, meeting his questioning gaze.

He shook his head as he stepped forward. Reaching out to run his fingertip along her cheek, he smiled. "Not me. You."

Her eyelids drifted shut as she leaned into his touch. She'd tried so hard not to, but she'd fallen head over heels in love with Cole Yardley. And if she was completely truthful about it, she'd been in love with him since the first time he kissed her. She'd just been too stubborn to realize it.

When she opened her eyes, he was looking at her

as if she really was the most beautiful woman he'd ever seen. Wanting him to see her as she saw him, she lowered her shorts and panties, then added them to the tangled pile of clothes at their feet.

He held his arms wide and she stepped into his embrace without a moment's hesitation. She wanted to feel all of him against her, feel the contrast of soft feminine skin to firm male flesh. At first contact, a searing current of heat seemed to dance over every nerve in her body.

She wanted him with a fierceness that astounded her, but the need to give to him as she'd never given to any man was more powerful than anything she'd ever felt. Running her hands along his sides, then down his flanks, she took him in her palms to explore his length and the heaviness beneath.

"Sweetheart, if you keep...doing that...I may never walk again." He spoke haltingly and his breathing was extremely labored.

"I've only just begun," she said, pressing her lips to his chest, his flat belly and beyond.

"Elise?"

"Shh, darling," she said a moment before she gave him the ultimate caress a woman can give to a man.

Taking her by the shoulders, he hauled her up to bring his mouth down on hers in a kiss that caused her to melt against him. The world seemed to tilt precariously, then right itself, and she realized he'd lifted her into his arms to cradle her to him.

"What are you doing?" she asked breathlessly.

"I'm dragging you off to my den again," he said, his smile leaving her with no doubt what he had planned.

He placed her on the bed, then tore open the foil packet with their protection. Rolling it into place, he stood looking down at her a moment. The undeniable hunger in his eyes was feral.

As he stretched out beside her, he turned her to face him, then lifted her leg over his. He must have detected her confusion. "I want to love you face-to-face."

Her heart swelled with love at his concession. Neither one of them would take the dominant position, but instead, play an equal role in their lovemaking.

Reaching down, she guided him to her, then in one exquisite move, he made them one. Her body sizzled as he filled her, and she could see by the expression on Cole's face that he was experiencing the same heated energy that she was. She closed her eyes to savor the feeling.

"Elise? Look at me." His voice sounded rough and she knew it had to be from the strain of holding himself in check.

When she did as he requested, he brought his hand up to gently cup her cheek. "I want to watch your eyes light up as I bring you pleasure, sweetheart. I want to know the exact moment when you can't hold back any longer and I take you over the edge."

She would have told him that she wanted that, too, but as his gaze held hers, he slowly began to move within her and words were not only beyond her capabilities, they were completely unnecessary. His gaze reflected the same unity of their souls that she was feeling.

Her heart filled with more love than she'd ever dreamed possible as threads of passion coursed through her to gather in a tight spiral in her lower stomach. His eyes never wavered from hers, and she could tell the same tension was gripping him, compelling him to find the completion they both longed to find.

Even as the sensations inside her grew to a delicious ache, she fought to prolong them, to savor the connection between them that she never wanted to end. But apparently Cole sensed her readiness, and moved his hand down between them to gently stroke her with his fingers. Suddenly the coil was unwinding, spinning her out of control. She heard herself whimper, then moan as waves of pleasure coursed to every cell in her being and she gave herself up to the tempest swirling inside her. As her body shivered from the force of it, she felt Cole's arms tighten around her, felt him stiffen, then bury himself deep within her one final time as he found his own liberation from the storm.

A sweet languor overtook her and she clung to his strong arms as they drifted back to reality. She had acknowledged that she loved Cole with all of her heart and soul, and if the look in his eyes was any indication, he had deep feelings for her, too.

That was the reason there shouldn't be any secrets between them, she reasoned. Two people who really cared for each other didn't hide things from the other.

She tried to stifle a yawn as she snuggled against him. She'd rest a little, then she'd tell him about the trip to Mezcaya. Surely he'd understand.

Nine

Cole smiled down at the woman sleeping so peacefully in his bed. Elise looked so soft, so sweet, it took everything he had to force himself to finish dressing after his shower and walk out the door. She needed her rest, and he needed to get back to chasing down the information to solve the gun-smuggling case.

As he drove to the courthouse, he thought about the night they'd shared. Throughout the evening and well into the early hours of morning, they'd come together time and again to share the most passionate lovemaking he'd ever experienced. They'd been so wrapped up in each other, they'd even forgotten about dinner.

At one point in the evening, Elise had mentioned that she needed to talk to him about something, but he'd kissed her and she'd forgotten all about what she'd wanted to tell him.

He smiled as he parked in the courthouse parking lot and headed into the clerk's office. There would be plenty of time this evening for them to discuss whatever she had on her mind. But right now, he had work to do. He needed to find out who held the deed to the warehouse property at the edge of town, visit the judge and obtain a search warrant, then go over those buildings with a fine-tooth comb.

Twenty minutes later, he walked out of the clerk's office with a satisfied smile. Why wasn't he surprised to learn that Ricky Mercado had bought the old warehouses a few months back? In fact, it had only been a matter of a few weeks after his return from the mission to get Phillip Westin out of Mezcaya.

But as Cole waited for the judge to see him and hear his reasons for wanting a court order to search the property, something bothered him. Why would Mercado buy the old warehouses to store weapons in, knowing full well that the ATF and FBI were all over every move he made?

It didn't make sense. Mercado wasn't a stupid man. He had to know the first thing they'd do would be to search every property he owned, and especially something as big as a warehouse where a cache of illegal guns and ordnance could easily be stored.

No, it was too convenient, too obvious. But Cole would bet everything he had that once he got access to the buildings, he'd find a whole arsenal stored there.

He frowned. That would mean that Mercado had been telling the truth all along about not being involved in the smuggling operation, that someone was setting the man up to take a fall.

But if Ricky Mercado wasn't behind the ring, then who was responsible for selling illegal weapons to El Jefé?

One name came to mind and it had Cole balling his hands into tight fists. John Valente.

Now all Cole had to do was to find the proof he needed to nail the son of a bitch.

As he approached the city limits of Mission Creek, Ricky Mercado tapped his palms on the steering wheel in time to the country music coming from his truck's radio speakers. In spite of the crap going on in his life, his trip to Nuevo Laredo just across the Mexican border had gone well. It hadn't taken him nearly as long as he'd thought it would, the hand-crafted Mexican tiles for his new kitchen were on order and would be ready for pickup in a few weeks, and there was still enough of the afternoon left to put the new railing on the back porch.

Of course, when Ricky started nailing the wood in place, he'd just end up pissing off the raccoon living under it. But those were the breaks.

That old cuss could hiss and spit all he wanted. He'd just have to get used to the idea of sharing his digs with a human again.

As he neared the warehouses he'd bought a few months back, the sight of a black SUV parked just inside the broken-down gate caused Ricky to slow the truck to a crawl. He'd seen that Explorer one too many times not to recognize it as the one Cole Yardley drove.

Now why in hell would Yardley be poking around those old run-down buildings? There hadn't been anything stored in them for years, and in another week or two they wouldn't even be there. They were scheduled for demolition and a new storage complex would be going up in their place.

Unless the feds had discovered something Ricky didn't know about, he couldn't think of one good reason for Yardley to be checking out the property.

Deciding to wait until the ATF agent had cleared out, Ricky drove home. He'd come back later and see what the man found so interesting about buildings that were ready to fall down with the next stiff wind.

Cole cursed when the cell phone attached to his belt started chirping. It had to be someone from the Vegas office. They were the only ones who knew the number.

Punching the talk button, he held the phone to his ear. "What?"

"I see you're your usual congenial self," Drew Monahan's voice crackled in his ear.

"What's up?" Cole asked, glancing around the cavernous warehouse. It was fairly dark, but there appeared to be a stack of wooden crates at the far end. He started toward them.

"We heard something interesting from one of our informants that you need to know about," Monahan said. The man's voice had taken on a seriousness that had Cole's full attention.

"Which one?" he asked, mentally reviewing which of their sources was the most reliable.

"Angel Sanchez."

Cole stopped dead in his tracks. Whatever the information was, he knew he could bank on it being one hundred percent accurate if it came from Angel. "So what did the old boy have to say?"

"There's been a hit ordered on someone getting too close to solving the case in Mission Creek," Monahan said gravely.

A knot formed in the pit of Cole's belly. The hit had to be on him or Elise. They were closest to the case.

The knot in his gut tightened. He wasn't concerned for himself. He'd dodged the Grim Reaper more than a couple of times in his eight years with the ATF. But Elise was working on the case, and although they hadn't shared the evidence they'd each collected, he knew she had to be getting close to finding the paper trail she was looking for.

"Did Angel say who ordered the hit?"

He heard Monahan's exasperated sigh crackle across the airwaves. "That's the hell of it. We've checked with every one of our contacts from here to New Orleans and all we've been able to learn is that the order came out of Mission Creek. We're still working on it, but it's going to take time."

Cole turned and started for the double doors leading outside. "Thanks for the heads up, Monahan. I owe you one."

"You owe me more than that," the man said. "But that's not important now. Just watch your back, Yardley."

"Will do," Cole said, ending the call. He started to call Elise, but the blinking light on the phone indicated the battery was going dead.

His heart pumping double time, he jogged the hundred yards to the SUV. He had to get back to the inn and tell Elise to stay put. She'd be safer there than out in the field.

As Cole drove across town to the inn, he thought about how much he should tell her. If he told her about the hit and insisted that she stay locked in their rooms at the inn, there was a good possibility that she'd tell him where to go and how to get there. Or worse yet, grab her gun and go out looking for whoever had ordered the hit.

The thought of that happening turned the blood in his veins to ice. No, he couldn't tell her to leave things to him. That would be the worst thing he could do.

But if he didn't warn her, and something happened, he'd never forgive himself.

Deciding it was time to call in reinforcements, Cole pulled into a parking space in front of the sheriff's office. He'd alert Wainwright to the latest development, and together they'd concoct a plan to keep Elise safe and out of the line of fire.

An hour later, Cole walked out of the sheriff's office feeling a little more confident about keeping Elise safe. Wainwright was arranging to send an undercover detective to the inn. A veteran of fifteen years on the Houston rackets squad, Jack Bennett had just recently joined the Mission Creek force and wasn't known by the locals. He'd take the maintenance job Mrs. Carter had been looking to fill, and stay at the inn under the guise of not having found an apartment since moving to town. Cole knew the plan wasn't perfect, but it was a hell of a lot better than doing nothing at all.

* * *

Elise nibbled on her lower lip as she tried to think of a way to tell Cole she'd be leaving for Mezcaya first thing in the morning. No matter how she broke the news, she was positive he wasn't going to like it. He'd told her on more than one occasion that he was glad her job kept her behind a desk and out of trouble.

Shaking her head, she sighed heavily. Just as sure as the sun rose in the east each morning, when he found out about the trip he'd go caveman on her, try to stop her from going, and they'd end up having a huge argument. And as much as she loved him, she wasn't going to shirk an assignment and end up jeopardizing her career with the Bureau just because he had a problem with her doing her job.

But maybe if she planned something special for the evening, she could find the perfect time to tell him and he'd be a little more understanding. She knew it was a long shot, but time was running out and it was the best she could come up with.

Picking up the phone, she talked with Mrs. Carter, and romantic soul that she was, the woman helped Elise plan an evening that she hoped Cole would not only find enjoyable and relaxing, but would also put him in an agreeable mood.

When Cole walked through the door connecting their rooms an hour and a half later, she and Mrs. Carter had everything set up in the gazebo and Elise had changed into a mint-green sundress. "How was your day?" she asked, suddenly unsure of her plan. He looked worried about something. "Is everything all right?"

"Another day, another dollar," he said, shrugging.

He took her into his arms and kissed her until she felt light-headed. "How was yours, sweetheart?"

"So-so." She grinned. "But there is something that I'd like you to take a look at in the garden."

His arms tensed around her. "What is it?"

"It's nothing to worry about," she said, stepping away from him. She waited for him to remove the holster and gun from his belt the way he always did when he returned to the room for the evening. But he just stood staring at her.

"What?" he asked, frowning.

"Aren't you going to take off your gun?"

He glanced down at his service weapon, then shook his head. "Not tonight. I...uh, may have to leave to follow a lead."

She smiled. "Would you care to share?" she asked, already knowing his answer.

"Nope."

"Then follow me," she said, taking him by the hand.

When they stopped at the registration desk on their way through the lobby, a man Elise had never seen was talking with Mrs. Carter.

"Here you go, dear," Mrs. Carter said, handing Elise the key to the door leading out to the garden. They'd arranged for Elise to lock the door after she and Cole entered the garden, insuring their privacy for the evening. "Oh, by the way, this is Jack Bennett. He's our new maintenance man. I'll have him fix that lock between your and Mr. Yardley's door first thing in the morning."

When Mrs. Carter finished the introductions, Elise smiled. She wasn't going to tell the woman that even if the lock was repaired, she and Cole wouldn't be using it. "Nice to meet you, Jack."

"While you're at it, would you mind checking the security chain on my door?" Cole asked, shaking the man's hand. "It seems a little loose and it wouldn't hurt to check Ms. Campbell's while you're at it."

"I'll put it on the list," Jack said, nodding.

"You two have a good time," Mrs. Carter said, grinning like the Cheshire cat.

"What did she mean by that?" Cole asked as they walked away.

"You'll see." Grinning, Elise waited for him to open the door leading out into the courtyard, then locked it behind them.

"Hey, what the hell are you doing?" He sounded alarmed.

"Relax, Caveman. I'm just making sure we aren't interrupted," she said.

"I don't think I like the idea of being locked in," he said, looking around the garden as if he expected to see someone.

She started down the narrow path. "It must have been a pretty trying day for you."

"Why do you say that?" he asked, following her.

"You're more tense than I've ever seen you." She turned to give him a quick kiss. "Will you at least try to relax?"

He smiled. "I guess I'll have to, since you asked so nicely."

The evening sun had gone down behind the inn, casting a shadow over the garden. She smiled as she climbed the steps to the gazebo. The candles Mrs. Carter had suggested would be perfect.

"What's this?" he asked, glancing from the picnic basket, to the candles lining the railing of the structure.

"I'm taking you on a date, Mr. Yardley."

"But—"

She placed her index finger to his lips. "It's apparent that you've had a hard day and need to unwind."

As Cole stared down at her, he decided that was the understatement of the year. Only he couldn't afford to let his guard down. One of their lives might very well depend on his staying alert.

"Why don't you sit in the swing and relax, while I light the candles," she asked, striking a long match and touching it to the top of each wick.

Lowering himself onto the swing, he didn't see any other choice but to go along with what Elise had planned. He'd just have to be especially alert to everything going on around them.

"What gave you the idea to go to all this trouble?" he asked, admiring how gracefully her full skirt moved around her shapely calves.

She smiled over her shoulder at him. "I just thought it would be nice for a change."

As he watched her blow out the match, then lift the lid on the picnic basket, he felt like the biggest jerk in the state of Texas. He'd kissed her. He'd made love to her. But he hadn't courted her, hadn't done anything to show her how special their time together was for him.

"Come here, sweetheart," he said, reaching out to wrap his arms around her waist.

Laughing, she allowed him to haul her onto his lap. "I see you're in caveman mode again."

"Something you do well, you should do often," he said, grinning back. "And you're always telling me how great I am at being a caveman."

She put one arm around his shoulders, then brought her other hand up to trace the line of his jaw with her finger. "I'm not going to argue with you about that. You do 'caveman' *really* well."

He kissed the side of her slender neck. "You know, sometimes being a Neanderthal has its advantages."

"And what would they be?"

He felt a slight tremor course through her as he continued to nibble at her earlobe and the sensitive hollow below. "I'm expected to ravish the woman I carry off to my cave."

"I'll have to admit that's something else you do *very* well," she said, sighing softly.

"Only with you, sweetheart." He leaned her back so he could gaze down at her beautiful face. "Do you have any idea how special you are?"

"Not me," she said. "You."

Cole shook his head. "No. I'm just the lucky guy you graced with your pretty smile." He brushed his mouth over hers. "You're the most exciting, passionate woman I've ever met, and I swear your kisses are addictive."

Touching her soft lips with his, he traced them with his tongue. He didn't think he'd ever tasted anything sweeter. He coaxed her to open for him, and when the tip of her tongue shyly touched his, his body responded in a way that left him dizzy. He was harder than hell and wanting her more than he'd ever wanted anything in his life.

No other woman had ever affected him the way Elise did. All she had to do was smile at him, or touch his hand with hers, and his hormones were off to the races.

He might have been able to fight the urge and keep his body under control, had she lain passively in his arms and just let him kiss her. But when she tugged his shirt from his jeans to run her palm over his belly, then up to rest over his thudding heart, he forgot all about hit men and the danger they both might be in at that very moment. Her fingers massaging his muscles, exploring his puckered nipple, sent a flash fire straight to his groin and made rational thought impossible.

Breaking the kiss to drag some much-needed air into his lungs, he rasped, "Sweetheart, if you don't stop that, I swear I won't be responsible for what happens next."

"Then don't be," she said, smiling up at him.

The invitation in her sweet face had Cole closing his eyes as he tried to resist the urge to take her right then and there. But apparently she had other ideas.

The blood rushing through his veins caused his ears to ring as she sat up and tugged his belt free from the buckle. "E-Elise, what the hell are you doing?" Her expression, the desire he saw in her emerald eyes, told him exactly what she intended to do. "I don't think—" he had to stop to clear the gravel from his throat "—this is a good idea."

She carefully lowered his zipper, then stopped to

give him a grin that just about sent him over the edge. "You're right. It's not a good idea. It's a great one."

Cole tried to remember why she was wrong. But God help him, he couldn't think of one single reason. He gave up trying. Making love with Elise had become as natural to him as taking his next breath.

He captured her lips with his and kissed her again, letting her taste his need, the hunger that burned within him every time he took her into his arms. Running his hand beneath her dress, he caressed her knee, her thigh, then brushed his hand against her panties. He slipped his fingers inside, and finding her tiny pleasure point, stroked her with infinite care.

Her complete readiness for him, the dewy essence of her desire, caused his heart to pound in his chest like a war drum. She lifted her hips for him to remove the silk and lace, and her complete trust just about sent him past the point of no return.

But when she lightly stroked the taut ridge straining against his briefs, he closed his eyes and clenched his teeth together so hard that he figured it would take a trip to the dentist to pry them apart. "Sweetheart, I think you'd better stop that real quick."

"Why?" She sounded just as turned on as he was.

He opened his eyes to give her a meaningful look. "Because if you keep touching me like that, I'm not going to last any longer than a New York minute." Catching her hands in his, he brought them to his lips to kiss each one of her talented fingers. "Give me just a second."

Setting her beside him on the swing, he fished his wallet from his hip pocket, opened it and pulled out a foil packet from inside. He shoved his briefs aside, then once he'd taken care of protecting them, he gathered her in his arms and lifted her to straddle his hips. The full skirt of her dress settled around them like a mint-green cloud as she eased herself down and her supple body took him in.

Cole felt as if he'd found the other half of himself. His chest swelled with an emotion he wasn't ready to identify, and tried not to think about, as he set the swing in motion.

The feel of Elise surrounding him, the passion reflected in her emerald gaze, clouded his mind to anything but the need to once again make her his. The gentle rocking of the swing, the moving of their bodies in unison, quickly had them both climbing the pinnacle.

When he shifted to be closer to her, he felt her tiny feminine muscles tense, then contract as she found the completion they both desired. Her climax triggered his own and his body shuddered from the force of it. Never had their lovemaking been more fulfilling, more poignant.

His breathing harsh, he closed his eyes and held her tightly against him. He'd taken a big risk making love to her out in the open, and if something had happened, he would have never forgiven himself.

He kissed her with every emotion he was feeling but couldn't express, then helped her to her feet. While she took care of arranging her clothes, he righted his, then blew out the candles.

"Let's take this to my cave, sweetheart," he said, picking up the picnic basket, and taking her hand in his. "I want to love you slowly the next time, and I for damn sure can't do that on that swing."

"I thought the swing was rather inspiring," she said, her smile sending his blood pressure off the chart and his senses spinning out of control.

Placing a quick kiss on her soft lips, he pulled her along as he made a beeline up the path leading to the inn's lobby. "I'll show you inspiring just as soon as we get back to my room."

Not only did he want to get her inside where it was safer, he wanted to love her in ways that the swing in the gazebo just wouldn't allow.

Ten

Deciding it might not be a good idea for his truck to be seen at the warehouses on the same day Yardley had been poking around, Ricky Mercado parked the vintage Chevy by the Mercado Trucking Company depot. Benito Pascal, the manager, was used to Ricky parking his vehicles there whenever he went out of town. Of course, that had been in the old days before he officially left the family and started trying to straighten out his miserable life. But Benito wouldn't care. He'd just figure, like everyone else, that Ricky really hadn't quit and had gone somewhere on business for Valente.

Ricky muttered a pithy curse. Like that would ever happen.

He reached into the glove compartment to remove a small metal flashlight, then got out of the truck.

Shoving the light into the hip pocket of his jeans, he set out walking the half-mile to the warehouses. When he passed the gas station—the *only* gas station between Mission Creek and Laredo, Texas—he made sure to keep to the shadows. No sense alerting anyone that he was prowling around after dark, even if he was going to inspect his own property.

The crunching sound of his boots on the gravel driveway leading up to the first warehouse split the night quiet and sent apprehension streaking through him. He ignored it.

He didn't spook easy. Never had. Hell, he'd walked through guerilla-infested jungles at night where the foliage was so thick it was pitch-black and he hadn't been able to see his hand two inches from his nose. So what the hell was wrong with him?

But tonight, something just didn't feel right. It was probably nothing, but he couldn't shake the feeling that someone was watching him, and had been since he'd parked the truck.

Narrowing his eyes, he stopped to scan the area. He didn't see anything, but that didn't mean someone wasn't hiding inside one of the buildings, or behind them.

He stopped at the missing door of the first building, and pulling the flashlight from his pocket, shined it around the inside. The beam of light disturbed an armadillo digging for grubs under a pile of rotting boards. But other than the animal lumbering across the dirt floor to get to his burrowed-out hole in the corner, there was nothing to see.

Still feeling as if he was being followed, Ricky continued to the second warehouse, alert to any movement, any indication that someone was lurking in the shadows. Just as he pried open the door to shine his flashlight inside the building's interior, he heard a dull thud at the same time blinding pain exploded at the back of his head. The light in his hand went flying a moment before he sank to his knees, then fell face forward. His cheek slammed into the hard-packed dirt, and the last thing he saw before he succumbed to the beckoning darkness of unconsciousness was the spinning beam from the flashlight where it had landed a few feet away.

"Wake up, you stupid bastard."

Someone slapped Ricky across one side of the face, then the other. Pain exploded behind his closed eyes and helped to clear some of the cobwebs from his addled brain.

"Wh—who…the hell…are you?" he asked, slowly opening his eyes.

His lids felt as if they weighed a ton and it took extreme effort for him to fight the lure of slipping back into oblivion. His eyelids drifted shut. Another pain shot through his head as whoever was trying to get him to come to slapped him again.

"Dammit to hell, I said wake up," the voice snarled close to Ricky's face. The man's fetid breath burned his nostrils and caused his stomach to churn.

Opening his eyes, the room spun dizzily and his vision blurred. When he finally managed to focus on the face in front of him, Ricky found himself staring into the coldest set of eyes he'd ever seen. Ice blue, they were the mean, heartless eyes of a killer.

''Why don't you just whack him and be done with it?'' another voice asked from behind Ricky.

So they were hit men. But who put the contract on his head? And why?

Ricky tried to turn, to see who the man behind him was, but he couldn't move. That's when he realized the son of a bitch held his arms behind his back. Ricky could tell that the guy was shorter than he was and struggled to free himself. But the man was stout and Ricky's efforts proved useless.

Turning his attention back to Cold Eyes, Ricky sized up his opponent. Cold Eyes was about Ricky's height and weight, and looked to be in pretty good condition.

''Who hired you?'' Ricky asked. He needed to buy some time, to look for an edge. If he didn't find one, he was a dead man.

Cold Eyes shook his head. ''That's none of your business.'' He doubled his fist and landed it hard against Ricky's jaw. Pain immediately shot all the way to the top of his skull. ''But he told us to mess up that pretty face of yours before we kill you,'' Cold Eyes said as he landed another blow, this time to Ricky's nose and mouth.

Ricky felt his lip split, then something trickle from his nose. The warm, salty taste of his own blood spread through his mouth when he tried to speak. ''Did the bastard say why he wants me dead?''

''It doesn't matter,'' Shorty answered. ''He paid top dollar. That's all we care about.''

Ricky struggled and tried to think of a way out of his captor's grasp. If he didn't get loose, and damn quick, he wouldn't have a chance in hell of surviving.

Seeing the next blow coming, Ricky turned his head and Cold Eyes's fist glanced off his cheek. The evasive move only served to piss off the hit man. Stepping close, he jabbed Ricky hard in the gut with his elbow.

The blow caused Ricky to fold and his sagging weight proved too much for the man behind him. When he dropped to his hands and knees, Cold Eyes kicked him in the side.

Ricky gritted his teeth to the pain and waited. When the hit man started to kick him again, he seized the opportunity he'd been looking for. Reaching out, he grabbed Cold Eyes's boot and pulled. As the hit man dropped to the floor beside him, Ricky rose to his knees to bury his fist in the man's stomach, then tried to get to his feet while the man struggled to breathe.

But Shorty hit him across the back of the head with something, causing Ricky to see stars dance before his eyes. He managed to turn and land a blow to Shorty's face, sending the man reeling backward into a pile of wooden skids.

His knuckles stung from connecting with the man's teeth, but Ricky ignored it as he staggered toward the door. The high-pitched hiss of a silenced gun firing, then the sound of a bullet as it whizzed passed his ear, caused him to tuck his body into a crouch.

When he burst through the door and out into the night, Ricky fought to keep from passing out. He had to stay on his feet and moving, otherwise he wasn't going to make it out of this one alive. Forcing himself to concentrate on putting one foot in front of the other, he automatically turned toward the lights several hundred yards down the road.

If he had one chance in hell, he had to make it to the gas station.

Elise blew out a frustrated breath. She'd intended to break the news to Cole last night about her trip to Mezcaya. But he'd been so determined that they weren't going to talk about their investigations that she'd finally given up. Of course, he hadn't really given her the opportunity to tell him much of anything last night anyway.

She smiled as she thought about how they'd spent their evening and most of the night. Cole had been obsessed with loving her thoroughly and completely, as if trying to reaffirm that she was actually in his arms.

Then, when she'd awakened this morning, he'd already showered and left the room. He had placed a note on his pillow, telling her how much he'd miss her and that he'd be back for lunch. But she'd be at the Corpus Christi airport boarding a plane.

Checking her watch, she sighed and opened the desk drawer. Since he hadn't given her the number of his cell phone, her only option was to leave him a note. Quickly jotting down the details of her trip, and when she'd be returning, she placed the letter in an envelope and sealed the flap.

Now, where could she leave it? she wondered, glancing around his room. Deciding that she'd rather not take the chance of him overlooking the letter, she grabbed the handles of her carry-on bag and stepped out into the hall. She'd leave it with Mrs. Carter. Elise knew beyond a shadow of a doubt that the kind-hearted innkeeper would make sure Cole got the note the minute he walked through the entrance of the inn.

"Mrs. Carter, would you mind doing me a huge favor?" Elise asked when she approached the registration desk.

"Of course I will, honey. What do you need?"

Elise handed the woman the envelope. "I have to leave town for a few days, and if it wouldn't be too much trouble, I'd like you to give this to Agent Yardley when he returns around lunchtime."

"I'll be more than happy to," the woman said, taking the envelope and slipping it into the pocket of her smock.

Elise had no doubt the woman would be poised and waiting when Cole arrived. "Thank you, Mrs. Carter."

"Think nothin' of it, child." The woman's eyes lit up. "By the way, how did last night go? Did that boy like the picnic out in the gazebo?"

Nodding, Elise just smiled. There was no way she could tell Mrs. Carter how much Cole enjoyed it without shocking the woman right down to the roots of her gray hair.

"I really need to go now, Mrs. Carter. If you'd see that Cole…Agent Yardley, gets that message, I'd appreciate it."

The phone rang, and as the woman reached for it, she waved Elise on. "Don't worry, honey. I'll give it to him as soon as he walks through the door."

* * *

When Cole turned the SUV into the inn's parking lot, his stomach knotted. Elise's rental car was nowhere in sight.

He took a deep breath and tried to remind himself that it didn't mean she wasn't safe. Wainwright's Detective Bennett was in place as the inn's new maintenance man, and he'd been told that if Elise left the inn for any reason, he was to follow her.

But when Cole entered the lobby and found Bennett standing behind the registration desk, he felt as if an icy hand had closed around his heart. "Where the hell is Elise...Agent Campbell?"

Bennett looked thunderstruck. "In her room."

Cole shook his head and headed for the elevator. "Her car's gone."

The detective fell into step beside him. "It can't be. I've been standing behind that desk ever since Mrs. Carter got the call that her daughter had gone into premature labor up in Houston." He stepped onto the elevator after Cole. "And there hasn't been a soul in or out of this place all morning."

"What about before Mrs. Carter got the phone call?" Cole demanded, punching the button to the third floor. "Did you see anyone go in or out before then?"

Bennett shook his head. "I've been in that lobby since you left this morning. The only time I wasn't was when—" The man stopped short, then cursed harshly. "Mrs. Carter asked me to go to the garden to collect a bunch of candles someone had left out in the gazebo." He shook his head. "I wasn't there more than five minutes."

When the doors to the elevator opened, Cole

stepped out and took off jogging down the hall. God, please let her be in one of our rooms, he prayed.

Digging his room key from the front pocket of his jeans, he jammed it into the lock and turned the knob. "Elise?" he called as he swung the door wide.

Nothing.

He walked straight to the door between his room and hers, then jerked it open. Scanning the room, Cole knew immediately that it was empty. Walking to the closet, he peered inside. All her clothes still hung in a neat row. He turned to see her calculator sitting on the desk beside a stack of computer printouts.

"Where the hell is she?" he asked, not really expecting an answer from Bennett.

Walking into the hall, he stopped to dig a cash-register receipt from his pocket. Turning to the man dogging his steps, he jerked the ink pen from Bennett's shirt pocket. "Here's my cell number," he said, scribbling the digits on the paper. "You stay here and let me know the second she returns."

"Where are you headed?" the man asked as he trotted to keep up with Cole.

"I'm going to turn Mission Creek upside down until I find her," he answered as he opened the door to the stairs. He wasn't about to wait on that slow-as-hell elevator. He had to find Elise before someone else did.

Twenty minutes later, as Cole cruised down the main street of Mission Creek, the knot gripping his stomach was almost unbearable. He'd thought she might have gone to the bank for more records. When he'd inquired about her being there, the bank president said he hadn't seen her in several days. The next place he'd checked had been the Lone Star Country Club, thinking she might have gone for a swim or a workout in the gym. But there hadn't even been a sedan in the parking lot the same color as hers.

Where the hell could she be?

Stopping by the sheriff's office, Cole advised Justin Wainwright that Elise was missing, and asked that he put out an APB on her. Once Cole had taken care of that, he called Bennett at the inn to see if she'd returned. She hadn't.

As he drove back through town, he checked his watch. Damn, he needed to search for Elise, but he also had to finish his investigation of the warehouses before the time limit ran out on the warrant.

He cursed and headed to the western edge of town. Once he got done giving those buildings a quick once-over, he was damn well going to find Elise.

Descending the portable stairs that had been rolled up to the side of the plane, Elise stepped down onto the tarmac. The heat and humidity were stifling as she scanned the small crowd of people there to meet the aircraft, but she was too excited to notice. For the first time in her career with the FBI, she was actually working undercover—something she'd wanted to do since joining the Bureau.

"Señorita?"

A man dressed in peasant clothes walked toward her. Short and wirily built, he wore loose, dingy white pants and an equally dingy shirt. Whipping his dirty white hat from his head in a gallant gesture, he revealed a cap of shaggy, jet-black hair.

"Would the *señorita* need assistance with her bag?" he asked, his accent thick and heavy.

Elise smiled and shook her head as she continued to look for the contact she'd been told would meet her. "I'm fine, thank you."

"Does the *señorita* need a guide?" he asked. "Jorge is *excelente*. Only twenty American dollars to see a red butterfly."

"No."

"Red butterfly is rare in Mezcaya."

"Thank you for the offer, but no," she said more firmly.

"The flight of the red butterfly is *muy hermoso*," he added.

She was beginning to get annoyed by the man's insistence. "I said no."

Leaning close, he lowered his voice so only she could hear. "Look, Campbell, you want to shoot me a break here?" he asked without a trace of an accent. "I've just given you the code words three times."

Elise blinked. She'd been so intent on finding her contact that she'd completely ignored what the man had been saying. "I'm so sorry."

She couldn't have felt more foolish. But when she started to speak again, a slight shake of his head warned her to be careful of what she said. Some undercover operative she'd turned out to be.

"No, thank you, Jorge. I'm not interested in the flight of a red butterfly. I'm on a buying trip for an exclusive import boutique and I'll need a guide to some of the local villages. Would you know where the villagers might be interested in selling some of their handmade baskets and pottery?"

"Sí, señorita," he said, grinning and slipping back into the heavy accent. "Jorge Cortez knows many such villages."

Relieved that she hadn't blown either one of their covers, Elise nodded. "Then you're hired as my guide and interpreter, Jorge."

Cortez grinned and reached for the carry-on bag sitting at her feet. "Follow me, *señorita.* Jorge will take you to Tierra del Loro, the land of the parrot."

Two hours later, Elise held on for dear life as Jorge steered his ancient Jeep around yet another pothole in the road leading up the mountain. They were going deeper into the jungle than she'd anticipated and she was beginning to wonder what she'd gotten herself into. But as they rounded a bend in the winding road, Jorge pulled the Jeep to an abrupt stop in a clearing filled with huts.

Her breath caught and adrenaline surged through her veins. Parked in the middle of the tiny village up ahead, several men had gathered around a semi. A small stack of cardboard produce boxes sat to one side of a trailer with Mercado Trucking painted along the side. The men were pulling heavy wooden gun crates out of the back.

Her attention focused on the scene in front of her, it took a moment for her to realize that the long barrel of an M16 rifle was pointed at her nose. Her gaze followed the barrel all the way past the butt end to the scowling peasant holding it against his shoulder. He definitely didn't look happy to see her.

When Cole walked by the second warehouse on his way to the building with the new chain and padlock, he immediately realized something was different. The door had been closed when he was here yesterday and the scrub brush in front of it was undisturbed. Today, it stood wide open and the brush in front had been trampled.

Taking his flashlight from his pocket, he switched it on and cautiously entered the building. As he surveyed the interior, the hair on the back of his neck tingled. The dirt floor had two gouges in the surface from the door to the middle of the big open area, as if someone had been dragged inside, heels down. The dust had also been disturbed off to one side—the definite signs of a scuffle.

He quickly unhooked the snap on his holster, ready to draw his weapon as he scanned the interior of the building. When he noticed a small spot on the floor several yards away, a cold, hard chill wracked his body. Walking over, he pulled a latex glove from his hip pocket, then knelt down on one knee beside the darkened area. He touched it, then shined the light on the dust and sticky residue coating the tips of the rubber glove.

His heart thudded against his ribs so hard it felt as if it might jump from his chest. The substance on the latex was red. Bloodred.

Careful not to disturb the area where the obvious struggle had taken place, Cole retraced his steps and went back outside. His chest felt as if it might burst from being unable to draw a breath as he pulled off the glove and reached for the cell phone hooked to his belt.

Had the hit man abducted Elise from the inn this

morning? Had he brought her out here to the warehouses? If so, had he…

Cole's mind wouldn't allow him to finish the thought as he punched in the sheriff's number. "Wainwright, call the crime lab and get a mobile unit out to the warehouses at the west end of town," he said when the man answered.

"What's up, Yardley?"

"We may have had a—" Cole had to swallow the bile rising in his throat before he could say the word "—homicide."

"Is there a body?" Wainwright asked. "Do we need the county coroner?"

"I'm…not sure yet," Cole said, fighting to keep his voice even. "I'm getting ready to search the area now."

Eleven

Cole looked in the mirror above the bathroom sink, hardly recognizing the man staring back at him. He reached up to scratch the three-day growth of beard covering his cheeks. If hell had a face, it had to be the one staring back at him.

His eyes were so bloodshot from lack of sleep, he looked as if he'd been out on a week-long bender, and the dark circles smudging the skin below made him appear to have two black eyes. He took a deep breath as he barely resisted the urge to bury his fist in the face gazing back at him.

He despised the man in the mirror. It was his fault Elise was missing. If he'd been more protective, more vigilant, she wouldn't have disappeared three days ago. She'd be right here, right now, in his arms where she belonged. Emotion rose up in his throat—the feelings so strong they threatened to choke the life out of him.

Squeezing his eyes shut, he clenched his teeth against the pain filling his chest. Why hadn't he told Elise how he felt about her? Why had he been such a coward?

He'd had more opportunities than he cared to count to tell her that he loved her, that she was the most important person in his life and that he wanted her with him always. But he'd put it off. He'd convinced himself that it was too soon, that it would only complicate things between them. But the truth was, he'd only been lying to himself. He loved Elise with all of his heart and soul, and he'd give everything he had for just one more day, one more hour, to hold her, to tell her how much he loved her.

Cole forced himself to open his eyes and take first one breath, then another. Walking into the bedroom, he sank down on the side of the bed and buried his face in his hands. Was this the way his father had felt when he'd lost Cole's mother? Had Gunny gone through this kind of hell?

If his father had felt even half of what Cole felt now, it was no wonder that Gunny refused to marry again. Cole knew for certain no other woman could ever take Elise's place in his life, his heart, his soul. And the rest of his existence was going to be a living hell without her.

When the phone on the nightstand rang, he jumped, then stared at it for several long seconds. He wasn't sure he wanted to know what news the caller had to tell him. The crime lab was still working on the DNA tests to see whose blood had been found in the warehouse. If it turned out to be Elise's, Cole didn't want to hear the words that would mean his last scrap of hope was gone.

It rang twice more before he finally took a deep breath and picked up the receiver. "What?"

"Yardley?" It was Justin Wainwright.

"Yeah."

"You sound like hell."

"That's probably because that's the way I feel," Cole answered cryptically. "What do you want, Wainwright?"

"I've got a little news you might be interested in," the sheriff said.

"Did you find Elise?" Cole asked, not sure he wanted to know the answer.

"Not yet." Wainwright hastened to add, "But hang in there, Yardley. That's not to say she won't turn up safe and sound."

Cole didn't believe it any more than Wainwright did. The contracted hit on someone getting close to solving the gun-smuggling case, and Elise's disappearance, were too coincidental.

He closed his eyes in an effort to stave off the devastating emotions that threatened to swamp him. "So what did you want to tell me?" he finally managed to ask.

"The preliminary lab report—"

"What about it?" Cole interrupted. "Does it rule out the blood at the warehouse as being Elise's?"

"No."

His heart sinking, Cole didn't care what the damn report had to say. "I'm not interested then."

"I'm going to tell you anyway," Wainwright said

stubbornly. "The forensics team found more traces of blood a few feet from where the scuffle took place. The preliminary findings are that they don't match."

"All that tells me is that someone fought back," Cole said tiredly. He'd expect no less from Elise. She was trained to take evasive action, to defend herself if at all possible.

"Right. Due to the signs of a scuffle, we already knew that much," Wainwright agreed. "But what we just discovered is that someone fired a nine-millimeter inside that warehouse."

"Did you find the slug?" Cole asked.

"Not yet."

"What did you find?" Cole prompted when Wainwright paused.

"We found a bullet casing inside the warehouse and several more outside along the gravel driveway."

"Sounds like someone was trying to run," Cole said, unwilling to get his hopes up. If Elise was safe, why wasn't she here at the inn in his arms, in his bed?

"That's what we figure," the sheriff said.

"Is that it?"

"It's all we have so far." Wainwright's heavy sigh filtered across the phone line. "Are you going to be all right, Yardley?"

Hell, no! Nothing would ever be right again. Not without Elise by his side.

"Yeah, I'll make it," Cole lied.

Lowering himself onto the swing, Cole propped his forearms on his knees and loosely clasped his hands. He had no idea why he'd walked out into the inn's garden, other than he had nowhere else to go. Wainwright had banned him from the crime scene yesterday after he'd driven the forensics team half-nuts, prodding them not to miss this or to look for that. And after the sheriff's call this morning to tell him about the team finding spent shell casings in, and around, the warehouse, Cole had felt as if the walls of his room upstairs were closing in on him.

But this had been a huge mistake, he decided as he looked around the gazebo. It brought back too many memories of the woman he loved. And the woman he might never hold again.

His chest tightened and he had to close his eyes to keep the flood of emotion from drowning him. He took one deep breath, then another. How was he ever going to survive without her?

"Cole, what are you doing out here?"

The sound of the soft, feminine voice caused his heart to slam into his ribs and made it impossible for him to drag air into his lungs. Glancing up, he couldn't believe what he was seeing, but he didn't dare blink for fear the vision of Elise walking toward him would vanish.

"E-Elise?" he croaked. He tried to rise from the swing, but his knees wouldn't support him.

Was she real? Or did he want to see her so badly, to know that the love of his life was alive, his mind had finally snapped?

"Darling, what's wrong?" she asked, hurrying up the steps of the gazebo. "You look awfully pale. Are you all right?"

Grabbing her by the arms, Cole pulled her onto his lap and held her to him. The feel of her soft body pressed to his, her hand gently stroking the hair at the back of his head, assured him that she wasn't a dream he'd conjured up—that she was very real and in his arms once again. A shudder ran through him and he sent a silent prayer of thanks heavenward.

He leaned back to search her beautiful face. A small patch of gauze taped above her eyebrow and a bruise on her chin were the only marks indicating the ordeal she must have gone through.

"Dear God, Elise, I thought you were dead," he whispered hoarsely.

She cupped his cheeks with her hands, then smiling, shook her head. "I'm so sorry you were worried. I might have been, if not for Jorge and his quick thinking. But how did you know?"

"Jorge? Did he help you get away?" Cole asked, pressing his lips to the bandage on her forehead.

"He was solely responsible for our getting away," she said, nodding. "I found out that I don't think well with a gun shoved under my nose."

Cole didn't know who Jorge was, but he fully intended to find the man and personally thank him for helping Elise escape. "I'm so sorry, sweetheart. It's all my fault."

"Why would you say that?" she asked, looking puzzled. "You had nothing to do with it."

"I knew about the hit men...but I failed to tell you," he said, forcing himself to draw in a ragged breath. "I thought I could keep you safe that way. Can you ever forgive me?"

"Hit men? Here in Mission Creek?"

As her words slowly registered, he nodded. "You weren't abducted?"

"Good heavens, no." She frowned. "Why would you think that?"

"When I found the blood at the warehouse—" Cole stopped short. "If you weren't being held by the hit men, then where the hell have you been for the past three days?"

"In Mezcaya. Didn't Mrs. Carter give you the—"

Cole suddenly set her on the swing beside him and stood up. "You're telling me you went to that god-forsaken place by yourself? A place where life is measured in terms of who has the biggest automatic weapon, and how well they know how to use it?"

"Yes, but I—"

"And I was stuck back here, thinking you had been hurt or killed?" he interrupted.

"I didn't know about—"

"Do you have any idea what could have happened? How dangerous it was to go to a country that's being run by a terrorist group as ruthless as El Jefé?"

Elise watched Cole pace back and forth in front of her. She'd never seen him more furious than he was at that moment. "If you'll stop firing questions at me right and left, and let me explain, I think you'll understand what happened."

"Explain?" he shouted. "How can you explain not telling me you were going?"

Her own anger rose like the mercury of a thermometer plunged into boiling water. "It's very simple, actually," she said, forcing herself to remain calm. "I knew you'd go caveman, just like you're doing now. But I did try to tell you."

"When?" He shook his head. "I don't remember

you mentioning anything about a trip into Mission Creek, let alone a trip out of the country.''

''I tried to tell you right here in the gazebo, but you had other plans that night.''

''You could have told me later,'' he said, his tone becoming a little more reasonable.

''You left before I woke up the next morning,'' she reminded him.

He blew out a frustrated breath. ''But didn't you think about the hell I'd go through not knowing where you were, or that you were all right?''

She rose from the swing to stand toe-to-toe with him. He wasn't going to hold that over her head. Not when he'd failed to disclose the information he had about a hit man in Mission Creek. ''You didn't bother to tell me there was a professional killer walking the streets.''

''That's different,'' he said stubbornly.

''Oh, really? I don't think so, Caveman.'' She poked his chest with her index finger. ''You purposely withheld that little bit of information from me. Besides, I left *you* a letter explaining where I'd be, and why.''

''Letter?'' He shook his head. ''I turned your room and mine upside down, looking for something that might tell me what had happened to you. If it had been there, I'd have found it.''

''You mean Mrs. Carter didn't give the letter to you?'' Elise asked, beginning to understand why he was so angry. ''She assured me that she'd give it to you the minute you walked in the door for lunch last Friday.''

''Mrs. Carter was called away on a family emergency before I arrived that day," he said, suddenly looking tired. He lowered himself onto the swing. "She's been in Houston all weekend."

Some of Elise's anger evaporated. "Well, that explains why you didn't know where I was." She sat down beside him. "But that still doesn't excuse your not telling me about the hit man."

"Our informant told us there was a hit ordered on someone getting close to solving the gun-smuggling case," he said. He rubbed his face with both hands, as if trying to wipe away the last few days, then caught her gaze with his. "I was afraid something might happen to you."

As she scanned his handsome features, it suddenly occurred to her why Cole looked so haggard, and why he'd been so angry. But she wanted to hear him say the words. "Why, Cole? Why were you frightened that the hit man was hired to kill me?"

He closed his eyes for several long seconds. When he opened them, her breath caught at the emotion she saw burning in their hazel depths. "Because I love you, Elise. I think I've loved you from the minute I walked into that El Paso field office two years ago. I was just too stubborn and arrogant to realize it until I thought I'd lost you."

"Oh, darling, I love you, too." Tears filled her eyes. "I kept telling myself you were too macho, too much of a caveman for me to even tolerate you. But the truth was, I fell in love with you at the same moment."

Groaning, he pulled her into his arms. "If they gave out medals for denial, I think we'd probably tie for first place, sweetheart."

"I think you're right," she said, putting her arms around his neck.

They sat for several long minutes, content to just hold each other.

"Would you like to hear about my trip to Mezcaya?" she asked, breaking the silence. She wasn't sure how he'd react, but she didn't feel there should be any more secrets between them. Not personally. Not professionally.

She felt every muscle in his body tense. "Yeah, I think you'd better explain about Jorge and that gun being shoved under your nose." He kissed the top of her head. "I'm going to have to decide whether to thank the man for saving you, or kick his ass for getting you into the situation in the first place."

Elise explained about Jorge Cortez being her contact in Mezcaya and about their trip to Tierra del Loro. "It's not an actual place, but more of an area where El Jefé has a stronghold over several small villages."

"And this joker took you into that hotbed?" Cole decided he'd better not ever meet up with Cortez. If he did, Cortez was a dead man.

"In all fairness to Jorge, he had no way of knowing that a shipment of guns were being unloaded in the first village we visited," she said quickly.

The blood in Cole's veins ran cold as he thought of what might have happened to her. "How did this Jorge character get you out of it?" he asked, not at all sure he wanted to know.

She smiled. "He told them I was a missionary from another village on the other side of Tierra del Loro, and that we were there to beg them for food to give to the orphans.''

''And they went for the story?'' Cole asked, touching the bruise on her chin with his finger.

''Well, not at first,'' she admitted. ''They pulled us out of the Jeep and demanded to know how we knew there would be food in that village.'' She shook her head. ''But Jorge told them we were going from village to village begging for anything that could be spared to feed hungry children. Then he pledged his allegiance to someone named Gonzalez and El Jefé, and damned the current government. That's when they let us take a couple of boxes of vegetables and escorted us to the road leading away from the village.''

''If it was that easy, how did you get the bruise on your chin and the scrape on your forehead?'' When she hesitated, Cole held his breath. He didn't think he was going to like her explanation.

''As we were leaving, Gonzalez showed up.''

Cole's heart nearly stopped. Gonzalez was a murderous, vindictive little punk, who had proven in the past he had no regard for human life. ''What happened then?''

''Gonzalez started screaming at the men who had let us go and ordered them to stop us.'' She shivered against him. ''That's when Jorge floored the Jeep and tried to outrun them.''

Cole swallowed hard. ''Tried?''

She nodded. ''One of the tires blew when he hit a pothole. That's when we had to abandon the car and start out through the jungle on foot.''

''Dear God, Elise, if I'd known that—''

She placed her finger to his lips. "It turned out all right, even though I stumbled over a vine in the path and fell face first into a tree." Smiling, she added, "Jorge knew where we were and how to get back to civilization."

Hugging her, Cole thought about how close he really had come to losing her. "Sweetheart, I know all this must make perfect sense to you, but I still don't understand. What the hell do vegetables for starving children have to do with gun smuggling?"

"I almost forgot about the best part," she said, leaning back to look at him. "I've got enough evidence to bring in a surveillance team to monitor John Valente and two of his companies."

Cole grinned. Nothing would please him more than seeing John Valente brought down and the Mercado crime family weakened beyond repair. "I figured it was Valente after it was obvious someone was setting Mercado up. What have you got on him?"

"When Carmine Mercado died, he left Frank Del Brio in charge of the mob. That's when Del Brio gained control of Mercado Trucking and Superior Produce. Then he died and John Valente took over."

Cole smiled patiently. "I know that much, sweetheart. But how does that tie in with the gun smuggling?"

Her eyes lit with excitement as she explained. "Superior Produce has been shipping fruits and vegetables to Mezcaya via Mercado Trucking."

"Let me guess," he said, laughing. "They've been hauling more than bananas and cabbages."

Nodding, she grinned back at him. "The weapons were hidden behind a facade of boxes filled with produce. When Jorge and I arrived in that village, El Jefé guerillas had just finished removing boxes of fruit from a Mercado truck and had just started unloading crates of M16s, handheld rocket launchers and enough ammunition to blow up Fort Knox.''

"And you saw all of this?'' he asked, glad to hear the end of this damnable case was in sight.

"Actually, I not only watched them, I took pictures of them,'' she said, her expression smug.

"So what do you think they'll get Valente on?''

"I know for certain they'll get him on money laundering, because he and Mannie Ferrar have been claiming more in produce sales than what's been shipped to Mezcaya,'' she answered confidently. "That's the way they've covered the money from the sale of the weapons. Then Mannie's been writing off huge amounts of spoilage as a way to clean up the money.'' She grinned. "I don't know what will happen when the surveillance team moves in to gather evidence on the gun-smuggling end of it. They may find enough to lock up Valente and his henchmen and throw away the key.''

"Wouldn't hurt my feelings if they did,'' Cole said, laughing.

"Mine, either,'' she agreed.

They sat for several long minutes, content to be in each other's arms again.

"Damn!'' he said suddenly.

"What's wrong, darling?''

"I hope I'm wrong, but I think that blood in the warehouse might be Mercado's.'' Cole tried to think when he'd last seen the man. "He hasn't been around since just before you disappeared.''

"I hope you're wrong, too, Cole." She looked worried. "I like Ricky."

"Oh, do you, now?" he said, raising an eyebrow.

She nodded. "I think he was the nicest anyone's ever been when I had to inform them that I was seizing their assets."

He grunted. "I have an opinion of that."

"Of the way I handled his case?" she asked, frowning.

He cupped her satiny cheek with his hand. "Sweetheart, I'm really proud of you. You're a hell of an agent, and I think you handled Mercado just fine." He smiled. "Only from now on, we'll work these cases together, not separately."

"But I didn't think you shared your investigations with anyone," she said. "And especially not a female operative."

"You aren't just anyone, Elise. I've waited for you all my life. You're the woman I love with all my heart and soul. Please don't go off like that again without telling me where you'll be and what you'll be doing. If something happened to you, I don't think I'd be able to go on."

Elise met his steady gaze and the truth of his words reflected in his hazel eyes took her breath. Cole really did love her, but he also respected and accepted her as his peer.

"I love you, too, Cole Yardley," she said, pressing a kiss to his firm lips. "And I promise never to go off like that again without telling you in person—not in a note."

"Fair enough." He kissed the sensitive hollow behind her ear. "So you love me, even when I'm a caveman?"

A shiver of pure pleasure skipped along every nerve in her body. "Oh, I don't think of you as a caveman anymore."

"You don't?" He acted as if he intended to throw her over his shoulder. "Not even when I take you to my cave and ravage your delightful body?"

She laughed and kissed him again. "Well, maybe there are times when I like having you turn into Caveman Cole."

When she started to draw back, he held her to him and tracing her mouth with his tongue, coaxed her to open for him. His taste, the feel of him teasing her with strokes that mimicked a more intimate union, quickly sent heat coursing through her and created an empty ache of need deep in her lower belly.

"Marry me, Elise."

"What?" She wasn't sure she'd heard him correctly.

"I just asked you to marry me, sweetheart," he said, his expression serious.

She wasn't sure it was the right time to tell him that she had a feeling she might have gotten pregnant the night the condom broke, but if they made their relationship work, it had to be based on complete honesty. And starting out a marriage with a baby on the way was something he needed to know about before they ever started making plans.

"Cole, I…think there's something we need to talk about first," she said cautiously.

He shook his head. "Beyond telling you that I intend to transfer from the Vegas office to one close to yours in Virginia, I'm not talking to you about anything until you give me a firm yes.''

"But—"

"If you don't say yes, I swear I'll go caveman right here and now," he said, his expression filled with promise.

"You wouldn't," she said, looking around.

"Try me." His grin left no doubt he meant what he said.

"Oh, all right," she said hastily. "Yes, I'll marry you. But I need to tell you—"

Her words were cut off when his mouth came down on hers in a kiss so tender, so loving that it brought tears to her eyes.

"Elise, I promise I'll protect and take care of you for the rest of my life," he said passionately. "Now, what is it you think we need to talk about?"

Taking a deep breath, her words came out in a rush. "I think I might be pregnant."

Time seemed to freeze as he stared at her for what seemed an eternity before he finally gave her a smile that melted her insides. "Do you have any idea how much it would mean to me if you are carrying my baby?"

"I'm guessing a lot?" she said, smiling back.

"Sweetheart, I'd be the happiest man alive." He tightened his arms around her, then immediately loosened his hold. His eyes wide, he asked, "Are you all right? I didn't hurt you, did I?"

She couldn't help it, she laughed out loud. "Pregnant doesn't mean fragile, Cole." Narrowing her eyes, she asked, "If I am pregnant, are you going to be one of those men who hovers over the woman for nine months?''

His smile was unrepentant. ''Probably.'' Taking her hand in his, he rose to his feet, then pulled her up to stand next to him. ''Come on, we have a few things we need to take care of.''

''And they would be?''

He supported her elbow as they descended the steps of the gazebo. ''We have to go to the courthouse and apply for a marriage license, then visit the jewelry store for a ring and—''

''Two rings,'' she said, allowing him to lead her up the path toward the inn.

He stopped to give her a quick kiss. ''Okay, two rings.''

''I want everyone to know you're my husband,'' she said, smiling at him.

Shaking his head, he swung her up into his arms. ''There won't be any doubt of that.''

''I can walk,'' she said, putting her arms around his wide shoulders. He carried her through the inn's lobby and over to the elevator. ''I thought you said we're going to the courthouse,'' she commented.

''Not before I take the woman I love upstairs to my cave,'' he said, stepping into the elevator.

Laughing, she nibbled on his ear. ''I love you, Caveman Cole.''

''I love you, too, sweetheart,'' he said, stepping out into the hall. ''And when I get you to my cave, I'm going to show you just how much.''

Epilogue

One week later.

When the alarm went off, Elise quickly hit the button, and slipping from her new husband's loving arms, tiptoed into the bathroom. She'd purposely gotten up an hour ahead of him in order to use the home-pregnancy test she'd purchased yesterday at the Mission Creek Pharmacy.

Following the instructions, she anxiously awaited the results. When the positive symbol on the test stick appeared, then became more vivid with each passing second, her heart skipped a beat.

"I'm pregnant," she whispered. "I really am going to have a baby."

She placed her hand over her flat stomach and clamped her teeth down on her lower lip to keep a nervous giggle from escaping. Cole was going to be impossible to live with for the next nine months. He was going to hover and fuss and drive her completely nuts.

Elise grinned. And she was going to love every minute of it.

But first she had to tell him he was going to be a daddy. And she knew exactly how she wanted to do that.

She dropped the test stick into the wastebasket, then opened the door and tiptoed back into the bedroom. When she slipped into bed beside Cole, he put his arm over her and pulled her close.

"Why did you set the alarm for such a god-awful hour, sweetheart?" he asked, his voice rough with sleep. "You never get up this early. Are you all right?"

"I couldn't be better." Snuggling against him, she kissed his bare shoulder. "I had something I needed to do."

He raised his head from the pillow to look across at the digital clock on the nightstand, then down at her. "At five in the morning?"

She nodded as she ran her hands from his wide shoulders, down his chest to his stomach and beyond. "I wanted to send my husband off to fight the bad guys with a smile this morning."

He grinned as he caught her hands in his. "If you keep doing what you're doing, I'll be smiling all right. But I won't be leaving."

"Well, we have an hour. I suppose we could..." She let her voice trail off suggestively.

"You do have a point," he said, lowering his lips to hers. "We could…"

He kissed her tenderly, and for the next hour he proceeded to show her just how he thought they should spend the time.

Lying in her husband's arms after being thoroughly loved, Elise felt like the luckiest woman alive. She had the love of a wonderful man, a baby on the way and the promise of a bright future ahead of them.

"Cole?"

"Hmm?"

"Could I ask you a question?"

When he opened his eyes, the love shining in the hazel depths caused her to catch her breath. "Remember, sweetheart, no more secrets. You can ask, or tell me, anything, anytime."

"All right." Wrapping her arms around his neck, she smiled. "What would you like to have, Caveman? A boy, or a girl?"

"I really don't have a preference," he said, brushing a strand of hair from her cheek. "If we find out you are pregnant, I'll be happy as long as you and the baby are both okay."

"But what if I'm *already* pregnant?" she asked, waiting for him to catch on.

His answering grin caused her heart to skip a beat. "Why do you think I stopped using protection as soon as we got married? I want to have a baby with you, sweetheart."

Smiling, she kissed his shoulder. "Darling, did you really listen to what I asked you?"

He frowned. "You asked how I'd feel if you had

already become…pregnant.'' His confused expression suddenly changed to one of dismay. ''Already? As in, you are? You mean when the condom broke—''

''Yes, darling.'' She laughed. ''That's why I set the alarm. I took one of those home tests this morning. You're going to be a daddy next spring.''

He sat straight up in bed to stare down at her. ''My God, Elise. How could you let me make love to you the way I just did. I wasn't nearly as gentle as I should have been.''

She sat up beside him. ''Relax, Cole. You weren't rough.''

''I know, but I didn't hold anything back, either.'' A muscle jumped along his lean jaw. ''What if I hurt you or the baby?'' He paled immediately. ''How do you feel? Are you sure you're all right?''

Laughing, she reached out to cup his cheek with her palm. ''If you don't run me crazy with your hovering, you're really going to be cute for the next nine months, Caveman.''

''Elise, this is no time for jokes,'' he said, shaking his head.

''Cole, we went over this last week,'' she said patiently. She realized much of his concern was due to his own mother having died from hemorrhaging after a miscarriage. ''I'm not fragile, nor am I delicate. I'm pregnant!''

''Yes, but what about the long hours you put in at work,'' he said, looking worried. ''You'll need to get plenty of rest.''

Loving him more than she'd ever dreamed possible, she wrapped her arms around him. ''That's already covered. I've decided to take a job with the

Bureau that doesn't require traveling. Then after the baby is born, I'm going to take a leave of absence.''

"Elise, I don't want you feeling like I'm pressuring you, but I can't say I'm sorry to hear you won't be out in the field again,'' he said, sounding relieved. He held her close and kissed the top of her head. "How long are you going to take off?''

"I don't know,'' she answered, pressing her lips to his chest. "Depending on how I feel after the baby comes, I may not go back.''

"That will be your decision, Elise. All I want is your happiness, and I'll do my best not to influence you one way or the other.'' He lowered her to the mattress, then leaned over her. "But I want you to know it won't bother me one damn bit if you do stay home to keep the cave swept out and raise our little cavelings.'' He brushed her lips with his. "By the way, how many cavelings are we talking about?''

She thought for a moment. "I think I'd like to have at least four.''

"Okay,'' he said slowly. "As soon as my transfer comes through, and I get settled into the office in Virginia, we'll have to go shopping.''

"For what?'' she asked, puzzled. Unless they'd be looking for baby furniture, she didn't have a clue what he was talking about.

"Sweetheart, if we're going to have all those cave-lings, we're going to need a fairly good-size cave,'' he said, grinning. "Preferably one with a garden and a gazebo with a swing.''

She grinned back at him. "I'd like that, too.''

His expression turned serious. "I love you more than you'll ever know, sweetheart.''

Happier than she'd been in her entire twenty-seven years, she kissed him until they both gasped for air. "And I love you, Caveman."

*   *   *   *   *

LONE STAR COUNTRY CLUB
continues in Silhouette Desire…
Turn the page for a bonus look at
what's in store for you next month!
THE HEART OF A STRANGER
by Sheri WhiteFeather
On Sale August 2003

One

Life was complicated. That much twenty-eight-year-old Lourdes Quinterez could attest to.

Her only ranch hand had returned to Mexico on a family emergency today, with no intention of coming back.

His understandable defection was the least of her worries, she supposed. Painted Spirit, the once-thriving horse farm she'd inherited from her grandfather, suffered from financial neglect. Back taxes had culminated into bank loans, and honoring those loans had drained the ranch's resources dry, making other debts nearly impossible to pay.

As the dry Texas wind scorched her cheeks and whipped her unbound hair away from her face, Lourdes entered the barn and headed to the granary to take inventory, telling herself to keep her wits. Her family—a surrogate grandmother, a visiting teenager and her own sweet babies, four-year-old twins—depended on her to make ends meet.

If only those ends weren't so frazzled. If only the farm hadn't gotten so run-down. If only—

Suddenly a shadow, a dark intrusion behind a pallet of grain, snared her attention.

She froze, hugging the clipboard she carried to her chest. Lourdes didn't scare easily, but the distorted predator, or what she could see of him near the ground, appeared human.

She preferred the animal variety.

A man in her barn meant trouble. Was he a drifter? A drunk sleeping off a hangover? Someone prone to violence?

She glanced around for something to use as a weapon, and spotted an old, rusted hay hook stored with several dilapidated boxes of junk in the corner.

Thank goodness for long days and exhausted nights, for being too busy to haul away the collected debris.

She inched forward and latched onto the hay hook, settling down her clipboard in the process.

The human shadow didn't move. But she did. Slowly, cautiously, silently cursing the shuffle of her timeworn boots.

She peered around the view-obstructing pallet and caught her breath.

The intruder, a broad-shouldered man slumped against the wall, was in no condition to fend off an attack, not even by an adrenaline-pumped female wielding metal prongs.

She moved closer. She knelt at his side, and for a moment their gazes locked.

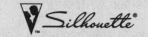

Silhouette

Desire®

presents

DYNASTIES:
THE BARONES

An extraordinary new miniseries featuring the powerful and wealthy Barones of Boston, an elite clan caught in a web of danger, deceit and...desire! Follow the Barones as they overcome a family curse, romantic scandal and corporate sabotage!

Coming August 2003,
the eighth title of
Dynasties: The Barones:

THE LIBRARIAN'S PASSIONATE KNIGHT
by Cindy Gerard
(SD #1525)

Is the heart of the carefree Barone daredevil, who rescued a beautiful, but shy bookworm from a stalker, now in peril of falling in love?

*Available at
your favorite retail outlet.*

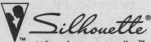

Silhouette®

Where love comes alive™

Is your man too good to be true?

Hot, gorgeous AND romantic?
If so, he could be a Harlequin® Blaze™ series cover model!

Our grand-prize winners will receive a trip for two to New York City to shoot the cover of a Blaze novel, and will stay at the luxurious Plaza Hotel.
Plus, they'll receive $500 U.S. spending money!
The runner-up winners will receive $200 U.S.
to spend on a romantic dinner for two.

It's easy to enter!

In 100 words or less, tell us what makes your boyfriend or spouse a true romantic and the perfect candidate for the cover of a Blaze novel, and include in your submission two photos of this potential cover model.

All entries must include the written submission of the contest entrant, two photographs of the model candidate and the Official Entry Form and Publicity Release forms completed in full and signed by both the model candidate and the contest entrant. Harlequin, along with the experts at Elite Model Management, will select a winner.

For photo and complete Contest details, please refer to the Official Rules on the next page. All entries will become the property of Harlequin Enterprises Ltd. and are not returnable.

Please visit www.blazecovermodel.com to download a copy of the Official Entry Form and Publicity Release Form or send a request to one of the addresses below.

Please mail your entry to: **Harlequin Blaze Cover Model Search**

In U.S.A.
P.O. Box 9069
Buffalo, NY
14269-9069

In Canada
P.O. Box 637
Fort Erie, ON
L2A 5X3

No purchase necessary. Contest open to Canadian and U.S. residents who are 18 and over.
Void where prohibited. Contest closes September 30, 2003.

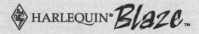

HBCVRMODEL1

HARLEQUIN BLAZE COVER MODEL SEARCH CONTEST 3569 OFFICIAL RULES
NO PURCHASE NECESSARY TO ENTER

1. To enter, submit two (2) 4" x 6" photographs of a boyfriend or spouse (who must be 18 years of age or older) taken no later than three (3) months from the time of entry: a close-up, waist up, shirtless photograph; and a fully clothed, full-length photograph, then, tell us, in 100 words or fewer, why he should be a Harlequin Blaze cover model and how he is romantic. Your complete "entry" must include: (i) your essay, (ii) the Official Entry Form and Publicity Release Form printed below completed and signed by you (as "Entrant"), (iii) the photographs (with your hand-written name, address and phone number, and your model's name, address and phone number on the back of each photograph), and (iv) the Publicity Release Form and Photograph Representation Form printed below completed and signed by your model (as "Model"), and should be sent via first-class mail to either: Harlequin Blaze Cover Model Search Contest 3569, P.O. Box 9069, Buffalo, NY, 14269-9069, or Harlequin Blaze Cover Model Search Contest 3569, P.O. Box 637, Fort Erie, Ontario L2A 5X3. All submissions must be in English and be received no later than September 30, 2003. Limit: one entry per person, household or organization. **Purchase or acceptance of a product offer does not improve your chances of winning.** All entry requirements must be strictly adhered to for eligibility and to ensure fairness among entries.

2. Ten (10) Finalist submissions (photographs and essays) will be selected by a panel of judges consisting of members of the Harlequin editorial, marketing and public relations staff, as well as a representative from Elite Model Management (Toronto) Inc., based on the following criteria:

Aptness/Appropriateness of submitted photographs for a Harlequin Blaze cover—70%

Originality of Essay—20%

Sincerity of Essay—10%

In the event of a tie, duplicate finalists will be selected. The photographs submitted by finalists will be posted on the Harlequin website no later than November 15, 2003 (at www.blazecovermodel.com), and viewers may vote, in rank order, on their favorite(s) to assist in the panel of judges' final determination of the Grand Prize and Runner-up winning entries based on the above judging criteria. All decisions of the judges are final.

3. All entries become the property of Harlequin Enterprises Ltd. and none will be returned. Any entry may be used for future promotional purposes. Elite Model Management (Toronto) Inc. and/or its partners, subsidiaries and affiliates operating as "Elite Model Management" will have access to all entries including all personal information, and may contact any Entrant and/or Model in its sole discretion for their own business purposes. Harlequin and Elite Model Management (Toronto) Inc. are separate entities with no legal association or partnership whatsoever having no power to bind or obligate the other or create any expressed or implied obligation or responsibility on behalf of the other, such that Harlequin shall not be responsible in any way for any acts or omissions of Elite Model Management (Toronto) Inc. or its partners, subsidiaries and affiliates in connection with the Contest or otherwise and Elite Model Management shall not be responsible in any way for any acts or omissions of Harlequin or its partners, subsidiaries and affiliates in connection with the contest or otherwise.

4. All Entrants and Models must be residents of the U.S. or Canada, be 18 years of age or older, and have no prior criminal convictions. The contest is not open to any Model that is a professional model and/or actor in any capacity at the time of the entry. Contest void wherever prohibited by law; all applicable laws and regulations apply. Any litigation within the Province of Quebec regarding the conduct or organization of a publicity contest may be submitted to the Régie des alcools, des courses et des jeux for a ruling, and any litigation regarding the awarding of a prize may be submitted to the Régie only for the purpose of helping the parties reach a settlement. Employees and immediate family members of Harlequin Enterprises Ltd., D.L. Blair, Inc., Elite Model Management (Toronto) Inc. and their parents, affiliates, subsidiaries and all other agencies, entities and persons connected with the use, marketing or conduct of this Contest are not eligible to enter. Acceptance of any prize offered constitutes permission to use Entrants' and Models' names, essay submissions, photographs or other likenesses for the purposes of advertising, trade, publication and promotion on behalf of Harlequin Enterprises Ltd., its parent, affiliates, subsidiaries, assigns and other authorized entities involved in the judging and promotion of the contest without further compensation to any Entrant or Model, unless prohibited by law.

5. Finalists will be determined no later than October 30, 2003. Prize Winners will be determined no later than January 31, 2004. Grand Prize Winners (consisting of winning Entrant and Model) will be required to sign and return Affidavit of Eligibility/Release of Liability and Model Release forms within thirty (30) days of notification. Non-compliance with this requirement and within the specified time period will result in disqualification and an alternate will be selected. Any prize notification returned as undeliverable will result in the awarding of the prize to an alternate set of winners. All travelers (or parent/legal guardian of a minor) must execute the Affidavit of Eligibility/Release of Liability prior to ticketing and must possess required travel documents (e.g. valid photo ID) where applicable. Travel dates specified by Sponsor but no later than May 30, 2004.

6. Prizes: One (1) Grand Prize—the opportunity for the Model to appear on the cover of a paperback book from the Harlequin Blaze series, and a 3 day/2 night trip for two (Entrant and Model) to New York, NY for the photo shoot of Model which includes round-trip coach air transportation from the commercial airport nearest the winning Entrant's home to New York, NY, (or, in lieu of air transportation, $100 cash payable to Entrant and Model, if the winning Entrant's home is within 250 miles of New York, NY), hotel accommodations (double occupancy) at the Plaza Hotel and $500 cash spending money payable to Entrant and Model, (approximate prize value: $8,000), and one (1) Runner-up Prize of $200 cash payable to Entrant and Model for a romantic dinner for two (approximate prize value: $200). Prizes are valued in U.S. currency. Prizes consist of only those items listed as part of the prize. No substitution of prize(s) permitted by winners. All prizes are awarded jointly to the Entrant and Model of the winning entries, and are not severable - prizes and obligations may not be assigned or transferred. Any change to the Entrant or Model of the winning entries will result in disqualification and an alternate will be selected. Taxes on prize are the sole responsibility of winners. Any and all expenses and/or items not specifically described as part of the prize are the sole responsibility of winners. Harlequin Enterprises Ltd. and D.L. Blair, Inc., their parents, affiliates, and subsidiaries are not responsible for errors in printing of Contest entries and/or game pieces. No responsibility is assumed for lost, stolen, late, illegible, incomplete, inaccurate, non-delivered, postage due or misdirected mail or entries. In the event of printing or other errors which may result in unintended prize values or duplication of prizes, all affected game pieces or entries shall be null and void.

7. Winners will be notified by mail. For winners' list (available after March 31, 2004), send a self-addressed, stamped envelope to: Harlequin Blaze Cover Model Search Contest 3569 Winners, P.O. Box 4200, Blair, NE 68009-4200, or refer to the Harlequin website (at www.blazecovermodel.com).

Contest sponsored by Harlequin Enterprises Ltd., P.O. Box 9042, Buffalo, NY 14269-9042.

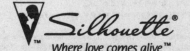

COMING NEXT MONTH

SDCNM0703